Election of the Undead

My Life Among the Undead:

Book 7

Camara M. Bragdon

***My Life Among the Undead* Books**

By

Camara M. Bragdon

Friend of the Undead

Yard Sale of the Undead

Secrets of the Undead

Carnival of the Undead

Holiday of the Undead

Reunion of the Undead

DEDICATION

This book is dedicated to my brothers, Tarren and Trevor Bragdon. Thanks for all your political insight.

CONTENTS

Chapter One:
Eddie Bravely Eats a Mystery Dessert

Who would have thought a birthday celebration could turn deadly?

The birthday party wasn't for anyone I knew. The big party was for Zephyr who was turning the big One Triple Zero. I'm talking about the city I live in. Not many cities can boast of being around for one thousand years. In a place filled with magic, a 1,000th birthday party for a city is no big deal.

Zephyr is a beautiful seaside town, filled with your not-so-average residents. Don't be surprised if you see a satyr, fairy, elf, or even a vampire walking around the city streets. Even a few humans are living here. Take my family, for instance. My father, my brother, and I came to Zephyr about six years ago through a wormhole from another world. We each acquire a magical ability. I'm a telepath, but I only have access to the minds of the undead. Sorry, where are my manners? My name is Shelly Anderson, soon to be Mrs. Eddie Van Helsing.

I was at my father's diner a few days before the celebration, going over our upcoming wedding with my fiancé. The very dashing Eddie Van Helsing was sitting across from me in the little booth we shared. The vampire scooped out the last bit of his broccoli and cheese baked potato before commenting on my suggestion about the flower selection I had picked out. I planned to put one fake flower in an empty, glass bottle for the centerpieces at each table. Simple, elegant, and cheap were the themes we were going for.

"Whatever floats your boat, Shelly," he told me, choosing not to look at me with his gorgeous green eyes. Unlike most vampires, Eddie is a vegetarian. Not by choice, but by some freaky genetic thing that makes him allergic to blood. He is five-seven, twice as strong as the average man, and has a head full of gorgeous, curly, black hair. He is also ageless ever since he was turned into a vampire over forty years ago at the age of 25.

I rolled my deep blue eyes at him. "It's not my wedding, hon, it's our wedding," I reminded him. I looked him up and down. He was wearing the standard uniform for the diner, a pair of black slacks and a royal blue collared shirt with the sleeves rolled up past the elbow. "Pick a flower!"

He closed his eyes and placed a finger on a white space between the pictures. He glanced at me and shot me a fanged smirk. "That one!"

I crossed my arms. "We're going for the invisible flower?" I asked him. A piece of my long brown hair had fallen in front of my face, and Eddie leaned over and tucked it back behind my ear. My irritation faded away. The vampire had that effect on me. The myth about vampires hypnotizing people is completely false, but this vampire could hold me in his "trance" all day long.

Eddie inspected my blue and white striped, short-sleeved sweater and my long jean skirt. "You're looking very exquisite, babe." He peered down at my brown, leather sandals. "New shoes?"

"Nice try in avoiding a decision," I told him. "Do you realize how many flowers I went through before coming down to these?

217!"

He rested his chin on his closed fists and placed his elbows on the table. "Whatever you pick, Shelly, will be lovely." Eddie wasn't totally absent from the wedding planning. In fact, he even offered to take care of the music on top of planning our honeymoon.

I rubbed my temples. Staring at pages of flowers for the past week was giving me a headache. A huge smile crossed my face. "I have a brilliant idea. How about this? We alternate between purple and white striped roses and metallic blue and white striped roses. We can order all the flowers on Dollar Town's website."

"Sounds like a plan," Eddie said.

A nymph walked over to our booth, carrying a newspaper under one arm as she balanced two plates filled with slices of a pie I had never seen before. When I say "nymph," I don't mean a woman with uncontrollable, raging hormones. I mean the mythological nymph. Nymphs are exclusively females, the daughters of satyrs and nymphs. Another interesting thing about nymphs is their surnames. When they turn eighteen, they take on their mother's maiden name as a sign of their womanhood.

Most people think nymphs are very voluptuous, blonde, eco-friendly, and known as airheads. Jazzie Birchwood was that exact stereotype. Her pale green skin glimmered under the fluorescent lights. Her long, platinum-blonde hair was pulled back in a very complicated braid. Two long, thin, green tendrils of birch leaves hung on either side of her head. According to her boyfriend, Strider Hornsby, it's her major flirtation device. The tendrils weren't getting the attention of every guy in the room. Her white peasant's shirt left nothing to the imagination. She was wearing a rainbow-striped wrap-around skirt tied so loosely I was afraid that one move of her hips would make it fall off. The sounds of her yellow flip-flops slapped against the linoleum floor as she approached our table.

"I'm in the paper!" she squealed at a pitch high enough to make an opera soprano envious. She set the plates down on the table hard so hard the pie pieces flopped over to one side as some kind of green and blue gelatin-like substance oozed on the plate.

I managed to swallow the vomit which was threatening to

arise. Dad had told everyone they could make pies for the diner's booth at the Taste of Zephyr festival, and apparently, the nymph had made something. "Really, Jazzie?" I asked, feigning interest. Maybe if she talked about her fifteen minutes of fame, I wouldn't have to look at what was on my plate.

She thrust the paper into my face and jabbed a finger at one itty-bitty paragraph down the lower left-hand corner. The minuscule headline read: Mystery Singer Heard Again. I began reading the paper aloud for Eddie's benefit, who was silently wondering if someone was trying to poison us. "'An anonymous caller reported to the Zephyr Herald she had heard the voice of QT. This is the fifth sighting of the rock star who had disappeared sixteen years ago. Other occurrences have included singing from an unknown source and a mysterious man walking around Bingington Square. Has QT come back or is it just a cruel hoax?'"

"Let me guess, Jazzie," Eddie said, "you're the anonymous caller?"

The nymph's head waggled up and down like a bobblehead doll. "Yes, I didn't want to tell the paper who I was 'cause I wanted to surprise Strider with my good deducting skills."

Maybe she should use those skills to find a recipe that doesn't look like it survived a nuclear holocaust, Eddie told me subliminally.

I kicked him in the shin in response. Jazzie was a nice person, but not the brightest crayon in the box, especially when it came to cooking. I'm a horrible cook and not afraid to admit it. Jazzie, on the other hand, was in denial. "Good for you, Jazzie. Are these pies you're making for the festival?" I glanced down at the blue and green-tinted white chunks that had freed themselves from the pie crust. Please say, "No."

"Yeah," she bobble-headed, "and Mr. Anderson said if Eddie approves the pies, they can be sold at the booth."

The vampire and I both looked at each other. Crap! Eddie said telepathically.

"So, Jazzie, what kind of pie is this?" I asked, bravely poking at it with my fork. I put the utensil down in case it suddenly disintegrated.

The nymph's smile spread across her face. "I call it Jazzie

Pie."

Eddie stared at the pie with concentration, but couldn't tell what the ingredients were because he thought his piece moved. "What's in it?"

"Oh, some hummus and tofu sautéed in eggplant and bilberry sauce."

That would explain the white floating lumps. I love hummus, but this was just nasty. "Is it—?" I almost said "edible," but I caught myself. "Is it good?"

"It's delicious! You should try some, Shelly."

I waved my hand. "No thank you, Jazzie. You see, I'm on a diet. Got to lose some weight for the wedding, you know."

"Shelly, you're not—Ow!" I cut Eddie off with another kick to the shin.

"That's too bad, Shelly. You don't know what you're missing."

A trip to the hospital. Stomach pumping. Oh yeah, I was all set.

She turned to Eddie. "What about you, Eddie? You're a vegetarian, and I know you'll love this."

"Well, I don't know, Jazzie," Eddie started to say, but the nymph interrupted him.

"Please, Eddie, Strider said you wanted to try one of my recipes for a possible dish at your wedding."

I raised an eyebrow at my fiancé. Really, in what dimension did you and Strider have this conversation?

He said she had a couple of really good vegetarian recipes.

You do remember Strider's Nuclear Power Plant Smoothie?

Ah, crap! I'm going to kill him!

Well, you might not get a chance if you eat that pie, I replied.

"Aww!" Jazzie said, "you and Eddie are sending each other subliminal love messages."

I looked at the diner crowd and noticed everyone was watching Eddie with anticipation of him eating the dreaded pie.

Eddie slowly took a bite of the food and nearly gagged when it touched his palate. He couldn't even swallow it, but let it swish around in his mouth. Tell her it's not quite what your dad's looking for, he told me.

I relayed the message and told Jazzie to keep trying. "Maybe you could suggest it to that new vegan restaurant that just opened up on Haywood Street."

"I guess I'm a misunderstood cooking genius. But you're right, I'll give my recipe to them." She cleared off the plates and handed them to a passing Weretiger waiter who was none too happy with extra dishes on his already full tray. "Anyway, I have a hot date tonight." She waved goodbye to us and strutted out of the diner.

She had barely walked out of the door when Eddie grabbed a handful of paper napkins from the dispenser and spit his food into them.

"Oh, that's just disgusting," I told him.

"Excuse me," he said as he washed out his mouth with my glass of water. "But did you have to eat it? I don't think so."

"Did it taste as bad as it looked?"

"Let me put it this way, babe: It would be a great interrogation tool. One bite, and you'd spill government secrets like there's no tomorrow."

"That bad?"

He nodded. "So, you're on a diet, huh?"

"Yes, I'm staying away from non-edible foods."

"Then why was I the guinea pig?"

"Because you're an immortal vampire."

"That doesn't mean my stomach's made out of steel."

"Just think of it this way," I said to him. "You just saved a whole lot of people from getting their stomachs pumped. You, my man," I said giving him two thumbs up, "are a hero."

"Wow!" he said sarcastically. "That makes me feel so much better now."

"Well, then I'll take one for the team next time."

Eddie crossed his arms and settled back in his seat. "Sounds good to me."

I decided to change the subject. "Who is this mysterious singer the paper keeps talking about?"

Eddie took his empty glass and began twirling it around in his hands. "QT, aka Quentin Tamself, was a crooner back about sixteen years ago. He was engaged to an enchantress who was his manager. One night after a concert, the stage crew heard them arguing. The next morning they both disappeared without a trace."

I leaned forward in interest. "What happened?"

The vampire shrugged. "Nobody knows."

"Were they killed?"

He shrugged again. "Like I said, nobody knows. The police spent six months looking for them, but they had to close the case because they didn't have any evidence."

I mulled that one over for a moment. "What do you think happened?"

"Don't know. She might have killed him with some kind of spell, but there wasn't any evidence to say what had actually happened."

"Maybe she turned them invisible or something similar," I suggested.

Eddie nodded. "That would explain the mysterious singer."

"Or perhaps she turned him into something no one would ever expect."

The vampire smiled. "That's a strong possibility. But what would she have turned him into?"

"Something that doesn't normally talk so people wouldn't realize it's talking."

"Like a tree or a rock?"

"Yeah, or some kind of animal," I said. Then I thought about it. The disappearance happened sixteen years ago, and I highly doubt our speculations were going to solve it. But it was still fun throwing the ideas around. Speaking of throwing things around. "Are we still on for my tennis lesson?"

He smiled at me. "Does tomorrow night at six-thirty sound good? I'll pick you up at your place."

"That'll work out fine. David canceled my lesson today, and Amelia and I are going to look at wedding dresses tomorrow."

"Sounds like a good plan," Eddie replied. He suddenly frowned. "Why did David cancel?"

"Didn't say. Why do you ask?"

Eddie combed back his short hair with black curls falling between his fingers. "It's just strange. He's writing a self-help book for new vampires and wanted my input on it. At the last minute, he canceled without warning."

I frowned. "That doesn't sound like David. It sounds like he's a little preoccupied with something."

The vampire nodded in agreement, but there was concern in his green eyes. "I probably shouldn't worry about it." He checked his watch. "My lunch break's over," He got up, leaned over the table, and kissed me. "I'll see you tomorrow night, Shell. Love you."

"Love you too, Eddie," I said, and then I remembered something. "Have you scheduled a fitting for your tux yet?"

He waved it off. "It'll get done. Don't worry." He gave me a little wave as he went back to work.

Right, probably a month before the wedding. I made a mental note to ask my dad to tell Eddie to get his tux fitted. I packed up my wedding stuff and shoved it into my small black backpack.

I walked to the parking lot and unlocked the small peanut-shaped car Eddie had given me for Christmas last year. Tossing my backpack into the passenger seat, I was about to start the car when I looked up to see someone riding on a winged horse about eight feet above the car. I sighed as I laid my head back on the headrest.

A few weeks ago, I had to give up my winged horse, Jordan, because she developed an incurable disease in one of her wings. The vet declared she could no longer carry a rider as it could injure her. I made a hard decision and sent her to a farm that takes care of retired flight animals.

I liked driving the car Eddie gave me, but there is nothing like flying on the back of a dragon, griffin, winged horse, or a giant bird. If you ever get a chance to go riding on the back of a winged animal, do it. It's an exhilarating feeling as you are carried high above the city and almost into the clouds. "Maybe I should get another winged animal," I said aloud to myself. Then I remembered my financial situation. "But it will have to be after the wedding." I started up the engine, turned on the headlights, and headed home to my apartment.

Chapter Two:
I Shop for a Wedding Dress and Eavesdrop

The next morning I left the house at eight-thirty. As I drove

over to my dad and stepmom's house, I noticed a wild griffin

flying overhead. Rolling down the window, I craned my head to

get a better look. Wild griffins were rare and potentially

dangerous. These creatures have the head of an eagle, sharp

front talons, and the back legs and tail of a lion. Their eagle

wings span about eight feet long. Because of the combination of

the two predatory creatures, griffins are vicious when not

domesticated. I quickly rolled up the window and drove on.

When I arrived at their house, my stepmom, Amelia

Anderson, met me at the door. "Shelly, how are you, dear?" she

asked as she hugged me. Her black hair was pulled back with a

silver hair clip. She wore a red V-neck shirt, white Capri pants, and white sandals. I, on the other hand, had chosen to wear a green t-shirt with purple flowers on the front and a pair of jeans that I had pulled out of my laundry basket last night. I did have the good sense to wear my gray sandals

"I'm fine, Amelia," I said as I came into the three-story blue house. The strong smell of fresh coffee and my dad's classic fruit pancakes drifted past my nose. "I take it Dad's up."

"Yes, he's going to be doing some yard work around the house while we're out shopping," Amelia said.

We entered the kitchen where my dad was standing flipping the remaining pancakes. He turned around and met us with his baby blue eyes. His six-foot-one muscular frame towered over my five-foot-six stepmother. She had to stand on tiptoe to kiss him.

I smiled at them. It had been a long time since Dad found love again. Ever since my mother had died when I was thirteen, Dad never dated until he met his next-door neighbor here in Zephyr, the widow Amelia Cross. It was love at first sight.

Dad looked up at me. "Good morning, Shelly. Want some pancakes?"

"Sure," I said. I purposely didn't eat breakfast, knowing I would be fed at Dad and Amelia's.

Using his ability of elasticity, Dad opened a cupboard door and grabbed a plate for me. "Have a seat, your stepmother and I were just getting ready to eat." Even though he hadn't been a cop for over six years, Dad still loved his cup of coffee in the morning. "Amelia, the coffee's ready."

Amelia, like me, is from my world and has a magical ability. With the help of her telekinesis, she floated three mugs down from the cupboard and set them next to the coffee maker. Then she made two cups for her and Dad. "Shelly, what do you want in your coffee?" she asked.

"Oh, I'll make it myself," I said. Both Dad and Amelia like their coffee flavorless with very little sugar. I poured myself some coffee and overloaded it with cream and lots of sugar.

"Who does she get her sweet tooth from, Timothy?" Amelia asked.

"Mostly from her mother, I think," Dad replied as we all sat down at their little kitchen table to eat.

"So, Dad," I said looking at his torn jeans and old T-shirt.

"Amelia's got you doing yard work?"

"No, I actually volunteered this time," Dad said with a smile. He took a bite out of his pancakes. "It gives me something to do while you and Amelia go look at wedding dresses. Oh, Amelia, Bruce called last night, and he's coming over to help me."

"Oh, good!" Amelia said. "Shelly, do you want me to call Libby? She's good at picking out the best wedding dresses. She helped me pick out mine."

"No, thank you. I think it'll be more fun with just the two of us." As a little girl, I wasn't one to dream and plan out my wedding. But one wish I did have was to pick out my wedding dress with my mother. Amelia is the closest thing I have to a mother, and I wanted her to feel included in her own stepdaughter's wedding.

"How are the wedding plans coming along?" Dad asked.

"Good," I replied as I took a sip of my coffee, "but we still need to decide on what flavor the cake is going to be. Brooke's making the cake. It's a toss between French vanilla, dark chocolate, and strawberry."

"What about a Neapolitan type of cake?" Dad suggested.

"Would that taste good?" I asked.

"Oh, yes! I made your father one for his birthday last year," Amelia replied.

Dad saw the hesitation on my face. "Or if you guys are thinking about a tier-type of cake, you can have a different flavor for each layer."

"That's a great idea, Dad!" I said. "I don't know why Eddie and I never thought of that." We finished our plates and put them away in the sink. We started to head out for our shopping excursion. Amelia gave Dad a quick kiss on the lips.

"Have a good time, you two," Dad replied.

"We will, Dad," I assured him.

After I parked in the very last parking space of the newly opened *Renfield's*, Amelia and I climbed from my car and made the long trek to the huge building about the size of a grocery store. The owner, Bianca Renfield, is not only Eddie's very sweet grandmother, but she's also the owner of Renfield's clothing, a multi-million-dollar company. As part of her wedding gift to Eddie and me, Bianca told me that she would pay for my wedding dress and make the dresses for my bridesmaids.

When we entered the dress shop, a tall, wafer-thin elf by the name of Sally greeted us at the door. "Hello, and welcome to Renfield's," she said in a wispy voice. She looked at Amelia and me. "You must be Shelly. Mrs. Renfield called this morning to let me know you would be in today."

"Yes, I'm looking for a wedding dress," I said.

"Well, you've come to the right place. Let me show you what we have."

Two hours later, I peeked out from the fitting room wearing one of the dresses. "Amelia?" I asked. "Could you zip up the back?"

My stepmother got up from her green velvet, high-back chair and helped me with my dress. "Let me see!" she said.

I turned around and looked down at the ankle-length white gown with the empire waist. The capped sleeves were embroidered with lace. The entire edge of the dress had an ivy pattern outlined with white sequins. "This is my favorite one."

She nodded in agreement. "You look beautiful, and I think

Eddie will very much agree when he sees you wearing this on your wedding day."

I smiled at her. "He'll love it."

After the dress shop, Amelia and I went out for lunch at the Blue Moon Café. Amelia ordered a chicken parmesan sandwich with fries and a diet soda. I ordered the same thing but opted for a root beer instead.

We talked about the design for the bridesmaid dresses. "I want the bridesmaid dresses to be versatile so the girls can wear them again."

Amelia nodded. "Who are your bridesmaids again?"

"Lisa's my maid of honor, and the rest of the bridesmaids are Gemini, Creighton, and Cricket."

"What about the groomsmen?"

"We're doing tuxes for the guys. Dirk's our best man, and the rest of them are Robin, Strider, and Tucker."

"What do you want me and your father to wear?"

"Well, Dad's wearing a tuxedo, and you can wear a formal. You know what? Talk to Eddie's grandmere. She can find a great outfit for you."

Amelia smiled. "Let me think about it."

I fished one of Bianca's business cards out of my purse and handed it to my stepmother. Then I excused myself and went to the bathroom which was at the end of a long hall in the back of the café. As I was leaving the restroom, I noticed two men sitting at a table in a heated argument.

The first man was my sword-fighting teacher, David Endora. Normally, the Welkie looks to be about sixty, but today he looked like his 300-years-old age. Welkies are a race of humans with various magical abilities. They also age slowly. When they use their magic for good, they are known as wizards and enchantresses, but if their magic is bad, people call them sorcerers and witches. David's iridescent eyes flashed in anger when he heard what his dinner companion said to him. "You can't be serious, Mayor Elfinson."

Mayor Magnus Elfinson was your typical Tolkien-like elf. Tall and elegant, the mayor was like a wolf in sheep's clothing. He had violet eyes and wavy blond hair, but he had a heart of ice. Nobody liked his policies since he was elected to office last year. He wasn't an evil politician. He was more like a lazy one who cut corners and did whatever he wanted to do. He did a lot of whining and threw temper tantrums to get his way. "There is nothing I can do, Mr. Endora."

"But that grant money was supposed to be only for Carpe Noctem!"

The elf shrugged helplessly. "The road crews needed the money more than your silly, little organization."

David's eyes flashed in anger. "The road crews needed to pave the driveway to your mansion?" he demanded.

The mayor shot a subtle, icy look at him. "You know with one word, I can have your organization run out of town."

David shoved his chair back. "I will find the money somehow, Mayor Elfinson, and you will regret your decision." He left the café without saying another word.

Chapter Three:
The Deady Sport Known as Tennis

As I waited for Eddie to pick me up for my tennis lesson, I decided to practice with my sword. Taking the red leather-bound book off my kitchen table, I slowly read the inscription on the front cover. "Knowledge is power!" Green magical sparkles began to fly around the book as it slowly changed into a sword in a red leather sheath equipped with its own belt. The magic book/sword was my Christmas gift from Eddie.

I had changed into a pair of shorts and a red tank top along with a pair of tennis shoes I bought especially for my lessons. I unsheathed the sharp sword. "En garde!" I said as I thrust the sword forward. The few months of sword-fighting lessons with David had made me quicker and stronger. I dodged an imaginary swordsman as I stepped back and forth and even crouched on the floor without losing my footing.

I barely heard the door open. I swung my sword at the figure standing in the doorway.

"Holy crap, Shelly!" Eddie yelped as he went into a quick crouch to dodge my sword. "You're dangerous with that thing!"

"Oh, please, I'm not that good," I said, modestly. "I just didn't hear you come in and reflexes took over."

"Yeah, just be glad vampires have amazingly quick reflexes." He was wearing a red T-shirt, showing off his washboard abs with a pair of navy blue shorts that accentuated his cute butt. The only downside to his outfit was his pair of ratty, old sneakers. "Ready for your tennis lesson?"

"I was born ready," I said. Walking over to the table, I activated the magic words to turn my sword back into a non-lethal book. "Without Knowledge, there is no Power." Placing the book back on the table, I grabbed my cell phone and keys and followed Eddie out the door.

Sitting in my poor excuse for a driveway was Eddie's car. Now, most people have this preconceived notion that vampires are incredibly rich and drive fancy cars. Not Eddie! This particular car is a two-door, carrot-shaped sedan. My fiancé is the best mechanic on this side of reality. He can fix and build any kind of car, and I mean, any kind of car. You want a car that pays homage to the Oscar Meyer Weinermobile, but can still kick some serious butt in a race. Eddie's your man. But his specialty is building ones in the shapes of fruits and vegetables. It shows off his warped sense of humor. I asked him one time why he had never built a coffin-shaped or a headstone-shaped one. His response? "Oh, please, Shelly, let's put me in a more clichéd role. Let me go get my cape."

We got into the car, and Eddie started up the car. I glanced at the green and red duffle bag in the backseat as I buckled up my seatbelt. The carrot car is Eddie's racing car, and he tends to step on the gas a little more than is necessary. "What's in the bag?"

"Some of my old tennis equipment," he replied as he took a sharp turn onto Gilbert Lane. "I'm a bit rusty since I played tennis in college."

I gave him a surprised look. "That was over forty years ago! You haven't played since?"

"Well, off and on," he answered as he turned on Prattler Drive. "When I worked for the Agency, I went undercover as a retired tennis coach to find out who was selling secrets to the Wixomite government."

"What was your undercover name?"

He hesitated. "Waldo Crimson," he said under his breath.

"You're kidding!" I said, trying to hold back the bark of laughter. "Waldo was your secret identity?"

"Hey, I didn't choose it. The Agency did."

I began snickering. "So, when you would meet girls, how did you introduce yourself? 'My name is Bond. Waldo Bond.' It sounds so suave and dashing."

"I'm so glad you find my undercover name so amusing."

"It makes 'Edgar' sound modern."

We finally pulled into the Zephyr Tennis Courts parking lot. Eddie reached into the backseat and pulled the duffle bag to the front, nearly taking out my head in the process. As we were walking to the telephone booth-sized office, the vampire security guard really didn't need to step from his office.

But he did, and now I have that awful image emblazoned

in my memory for the rest of my life. His "uniform" consisted of a green shirt tight enough to show off his steroid-pumped muscles equipped with a clipped plastic, handwritten name badge declaring "Officer of the Tennis Court, Ken." His matching green shorts were a reminder of why short shorts went out of style.

"We signed up to use the courts," Eddie told him.

Ken flipped through the two sheets of paper attached to his clipboard. "Name?" he demanded in a rent-a-cop voice.

"Eddie Van Helsing."

Ken glanced back down at his clipboard and nodded. "Can I see some identification?"

"Are you serious?" I said. "It's a tennis court."

"Listen, little lady, on these courts, I'm the law."

I glanced over the courts. The nice lighting on the free, public-use tennis courts was the only thing going for it. The green color of the asphalt had lost its luster from years of use. Even the waist-high net had at least ten patched-up holes. Clearly, this place was a hard-hit crime area.

Eddie fished his wallet from his shorts pocket and showed Ken his ID.

"You didn't mention you would be bringing a guest," the guard replied.

"I thought that was a given," Eddie answered.

"Did you think he'd be playing doubles with the invisible man?" I asked.

Ken sauntered back to his office and returned with a two-inch thick book thrown together in a three-ring binder. He began flipping through it. He found what he was looking for. "Here is it!" he shouted, nearly shoving the book in our faces. "Rule 749: Section 5h. 'In order to reserve use of the courts, the person making the reservation must state the name, age, and gender of the players,'" he recited from memory.

"Is that necessary?" I asked.

"It is because I have to make sure you're not in any danger, especially from him," he replied, glancing over at Eddie. He gave me a not-too-subtle wink which made it look like his eye was twitching. "It's my job to keep all the ladies from danger."

"He's not the one you should be worried about," I said, indicating I was the one not to be tangled with.

Ken didn't get the hint. "Before you play, you must read

and memorize all of the rules."

"You've got to be kidding!" I replied. "We can't read this! It'll take us all night."

I didn't want to deal with this idiot any longer than necessary. "So, have you memorized the rules?" I challenged him. It didn't take any special powers to figure out that this self-appointed tyrant of the tennis court was the author of the rule book.

"Of course, I have!" Ken said haughtily. "In fact, I wrote them!"

Theory confirmed, I said to Eddie.

He nodded with a roll of his eyes.

I opened a random page in the book. "So, what does Rule Number 57: Section 3e say?"

"Well-Um-Eh!" he stammered.

"It says, 'Players cannot, under any circumstances, bring food or drink onto the courts. Doing so will result in lifetime banishment from the tennis courts.'"

"Of course, it does!"

"If you can't remember every rule in your stupid rulebook,

then don't expect us to know them," I replied as I chucked the three-ring binder back at Ken. The book crashed to the floor and papers went everywhere. The vampire scrambled to pick them up as Eddie and I walked onto the court.

Dropping the duffle bag on one of the semi-non-sticky bleachers, Eddie unzipped it and pulled out two tennis rackets and a brand-new tennis ball. "how was dress shopping?" he asked as he tossed me a racket.

"Great, I found one!"

"So, what's it look like? Do you have pictures?"

"I can't tell you!" I protested with a smile.

"And why not?"

"Tradition," I replied. "The groom can't see the bride in her dress."

"Screw tradition!" he said, grabbing me by the waist and giving me a passionate kiss. "I want to see that dress on you."

I threw my arms around his neck and returned the kiss. "Sorry, sweetie, but you're going to have to wait until September 18. But I will give you one hint: It is the same style as the dress I wore at your grandmere's gala."

He wrinkled his brow. "Which one was that?"

I smiled mysteriously at him. "That's for me to know, and you to find out."

He let go of me. "All right, I guess I'll have to wait until our wedding."

"Yep!" I swung the racquet a couple of times. "And just to impress you, I did some research on tennis." I walked over to the left side of the net. "And I'm ready to play!"

Eddie walked to the other side of the net with the ball and the racquet. He arched his back and served the ball towards me. The yellow ball flew up in the air, saw me, and did a nosedive right for the top of my skull. What I did next was out of pure instinct and terror. Throwing my racquet above my head, I hunkered down and braced for impact with a scream Janet Leigh couldn't match.

"What the heck was that?" Eddie asked as the ball bounced off my arm and onto the ground.

"The ball was going to kill me!" I was still hunkering down.

"Really?"

"Yes, it has it out for me. It must be enchanted or

something."

"Shelly, I assure you these balls aren't enchanted."

"Well, they must be, and you just can't sense the magic."

"You're only a foot away from the net," Eddie pointed out.

I looked at the net and backed up a couple of feet. He was right. I was almost kissing the net. I was that close. I retrieved the ball and tossed it back to him. "Okay, I'm ready this time."

Eddie served the ball to me. "Good hit, babe!" he said as it hit the racquet. Then he winced as it bounced off the net and nailed me right in the shin.

"Ow! Ow!" I clutched my shin as I fell to the ground.

The vampire ran around to my side of the court to help me to my feet. "I don't think you're holding it right."

"Could you show me?"

"So much for your research." He pressed his body close to mine. "Stand sideways with your knees slightly bent."

"Like this?" I asked as I attempted to mimic his movements.

"You got it."

I felt his left hand touch my forearm as he showed me

how to properly hold the racquet in my right hand. He leaned in close to my ear, and I expected him to say something seductive, but was sorely disappointed when he said, "Now, picture the ball coming straight for you, and—." He paused and looked up. His green eyes darted around the court, looking for someone or something.

"What's wrong?" I asked. I strained my eyes against the darkness past the street lights.

Did you hear something?

No. He signaled me to wait and listen. Then I heard it. The faint clicking of what sounded like the shutter on a camera. *I did hear it this time*, I telepathically told him. *It sounds like someone taking pictures. Is that what you heard?*

That's what I thought. I'm going to take a quick look around.

I joined him, and we walked the perimeter of the court. Nothing or nobody showed up. "Why would somebody be taking pictures?" I asked in a whisper.

Eddie shrugged. "Don't know," he replied. "I'll ask Ken. Maybe he saw something." He walked over to the office and asked the "guard" if he saw anyone taking pictures.

Ken quickly put his bodybuilding magazine down on the table. "It wasn't me, I swear. Those days are gone."

"Okay," Eddie said, really not wanting to pursue that subject any further. "I just wanted to know if you saw anyone taking pictures of us."

"Why? Are you hiding something? Getting all kinky with her?" He waggled his eyebrows at me.

My fiancé rolled his eyes. "No! You know what? Forget I even asked."

We walked back to the center of the court. "That went well."

"I don't know why I even bothered. The guy's a complete moron." Eddie shook his head in disgust. "Shall we get back to the lesson?"

"Of course!" I replied. "So, how should I hit the ball?"

Eddie thought for a moment, and then he smiled as an idea came to him. "Well, swing the racquet as you would your sword."

"You mean Knowledge I named my sword Knowledge."

"You named your sword?"

"Yeah, it's easier than saying, 'my sword.' Plus, if I need to use it on the spur, I can just say something about knowing to catch the bad guy off guard."

"You've really thought about this, haven't you?"

"Okay, I might have spent a little too much time on it," I admitted.

"I think it's pretty cool," he replied as he gave me a quick kiss. He walked over to the opposite side of the net. "Ready?" he asked. Once he saw my nod, he served the ball.

Swing the racquet as I would my sword, I repeated Eddie's instructions silently as I prepared myself to play by moving back and forth on the court with my knees slightly bent. The ball sailed toward me, and I gave it a good hard WHACK with my racquet. The ball and my racquet flew out in front of me. I heard a yelp as Eddie dodged the oncoming racquet. He stumbled backward and fell onto his butt. I gasped and ran over to my fiancé's side. "Ohmigod! Are you okay, hon?"

Eddie was recovering from the sudden scare by lying on the ground. "Congratulations, Shelly. You're the first person in history who has nearly succeeded in decapitating a vampire with a tennis racquet."

"I'm so sorry!" I grabbed his hands and pulled him to his feet. "You're not hurt, are you?"

Eddie shook his head. "I'm fine, babe." He put an arm around me. "Don't worry about it."

"I'm a horrible tennis player," I whined.

"What do you mean? This is your first lesson. You'll get better."

"Let's see," I said as I started to count off my fingers. "I cowered from the ball, I nailed my shin with the ball, and I nearly killed my future husband with a tennis racquet. How many tennis players have done that on their first lesson?"

"You're being too hard on yourself, Shell."

"Well, it's just that everyone in my family has great athletic ability, and I don't!"

"But you're the only one in your family who can kick butt with a sword, and I don't think your dad or Robin can top that."

I sighed. "You're right, but I kind of wanted to see if I could succeed at an actual sport."

"You want to do another lesson in a couple of weeks?" I nodded. We gathered up our equipment, told Ken we were done for the night and got into Eddie's car. As he started up the engine, I remembered what happened at the restaurant. "Eddie, something weird happened earlier," I said.

He pulled into traffic before looking over at me. "What?"

"Well, Amelia and I went to the Blue Moon Café for lunch, and I saw David there with the mayor."

"So?"

"They were having a heated argument."

Eddie gave me a suspicious glance. "Were you eavesdropping?"

"Well, their table was right next to the bathrooms."

He blew out a sigh. He shouldn't have been so surprised. This wasn't the first time I "accidentally" eavesdropped on a conversation. "So, what was their argument about?"

"They're cutting the funding for Carpe Noctem."

Eddie nearly veered off the road as he looked at me in shock. "They can't do that! Carpe Noctem has helped a lot of people. I don't know where I would be today if Carpe Noctem hadn't found me on the streets."

I put a hand on his forearm. "I know, hon."

"Carpe Noctem is run solely on grant money, and donations, and paid out of David's own pocket. Plus, he just opened up the building on Yetta Street. Without the grant money, the Zephyr-area Carpe Noctem can't operate."

"That's just what I heard, and David was very upset about it. He told the mayor he would find the money somehow, and that the mayor would regret his decision. Then he stalked out of the restaurant."

Eddie sighed as he pulled into my driveway. He put the car into park and we sat in silence for a few minutes as the vampire took in the information I just delivered. "You know what? David has been my mentor ever since I became a vampire. He got me into the Agency when I had little experience in surveillance work. He has always been there for me, even when I lost some of my jobs. I wish I could help him out financially, but we have to watch our budget for the wedding." He paused for a moment and then looked at me. "I've been thinking about the wedding ceremony, and if it's alright with you, I want to ask David to be the officiant.”

“Of course, Eddie. And we should ask him together.”

The vampire grinned, his curved fangs gleaming in the moonlight. “That’s just what I was thinking! We have to ask him at the end of the week. That’s the only night I’m free. We’re going to the grand opening of Carpe Noctum tomorrow night, and the guys and I are playing poker afterward. Then we have the festival the next night, the first ball game of the season the night after that, and we’ll have to ask him the following night.”

I nodded, not realizing how busy of a week it was going to be. I leaned forward and kissed him. “Good night, honey.”

He ran his fingers through my hair and kissed me back. “Good night, babe,” he said softly.

I grinned at him as we got out of the car. He walked me to my door, and we kissed again. As I watched Eddie drive off, I slowly began counting down the days when we would be spending our days and nights together.

Chapter Four:
David Shows Off Zephyr's New Carpe Noctum

Disturbing images filled my dreams. People screaming as they ran for their lives from an unknown terror. Rivers of blood flowing from David's prone body. The dreams vanished as I woke up at the ungodly hour of five o'clock in the morning.

After a fruitless ten minutes of trying to fall back asleep, I dragged my butt out of bed and into the shower. While I ate a filling breakfast of a bagel topped with cream cheese and a cup of coffee, I began to read the Zephyr Herald. The front page headline talked about the upcoming festival activities. I made a mental note on the time for the Taste of Zephyr, from 5-9 pm. Then I flipped through the rest of the paper until I saw the headline on the section of the city gossip page, aka the Zephyr Buzz: Vampire Gets Frisky with Diner Owner's Daughter. Plastered right underneath it for all to see was an altered picture of Eddie showing me how to swing the tennis racquet. In reality, Eddie's hand had been on my forearm, but now it looked like he had his hand in my shorts.

"What is Miss Shelly Anderson teaching the children of Zephyr by this portrayal of illicit behavior? Last night at the city's tennis courts, Miss Anderson was caught in the act with Eddie Van Helsing, a wandering vampire with a mysterious past," the article read. "Her father, Timothy Anderson, has had enough trouble settling into Zephyr with his alleged dealings with black magic. Now his daughter is gallivanting about with an ageless bloodsucker." My temper began to rise as I read the rest of the article. Nothing good ever came from the mouth of Barbie Spellman, a hard-core, gossip columnist witch who uses her magic to get the story, no matter what the truth is. Furious, I grabbed my cell phone and dialed my favorite number.

Three rings later, I heard a groggy "Hello?"

"Eddie, have you read the paper?"

"Shelly, do you realize what time it is?"

I glanced at my watch. "It's only seven-thirty."

"Precisely! I went to bed two hours ago. So, the town must

be burning down for you to wake me up.”

“Oh, it will be once you read the paper.”

He grunted as he got out of bed. I heard him open his bedroom door and walk down the stairs. “If I get sunburned, I’m blaming you.” I heard him open the front door, grab the paper, and slam it shut again. He yawned as he rustled through the paper. “You woke me up for the festival information?”

I shook my head. “No, the headline of the Zephyr Buzz.” The paper rustled some more, and then there was silence for a minute or so. “Okay?”

“Did you read the headline and look at the picture?”

“Holy smokes! My hand wasn’t even in that vicinity.”

“Exactly!”

“And did you see who wrote this scandalous article?”

“Barbie Spellman? Why does that name ring a bell?”

“She was the hag who accused Dad of using black magic to get rid of those Level Five demons,” I said bitterly.

“Oh,” Eddie said, finally understanding.

“You know what I am going to do when I get out of work?” Not giving the vampire time to answer, I continued seething, “I’m going to give her a piece of my mind."

"Shelly, do not—and I mean it—go after her with your sword."

"But, Eddie, she portrayed me as a slut!"

"Yes, and I'm sure that running her through with your sword isn't going to help your image." He blew out a sigh. "Look, everyone knows we're engaged, and nobody reads the gossip section anyway."

"You'd be surprised," I muttered under my breath.

"I think you're overreacting. If anyone mentions it, both you and I will talk to her tonight after we go to David's open house."

"And set her straight?"

"With minimal bloodshed, hopefully."

I gave a reluctant sigh. "Okay, I won't go ballistic. Much!"

"Thank God," Eddie said with a yawn. "I'm going back to bed. Pick you up from work?"

"Yeah," I replied.

"Love you, babe."

"Love you, sweetie." I hung up and placed my phone in

my purse. Since there was nothing else to do, I made my lunch and worked on possible menu choices for the reception. By the time I left the house, I had narrowed down the food to ten choices, five vegetarian and five meat. Eddie would have to help me with the rest.

Fortunately, none of my library coworkers and none of my normal patrons read the Zephyr Buzz, and so Barbie Spellman was saved from my wrath, for the time being. My shift finished at five, and I walked out with my coworkers. Eddie was leaning against his green motorcycle, our helmets hanging off one of the handlebars. He wore a black blazer over a red short-sleeved shirt and a pair of brand-new black jeans. "Good afternoon, Shell," he said as he kissed me.

I wore a dark green sleeveless dress shirt and black casual pants with my work sneakers. "Can we swing by my house? I want to change into my black dress shoes."

"Sure," Eddie replied as he took my purse and placed it in the little box on the back of the bike.

I secured my helmet and straddled the motorcycle. Once

my fiancé had strapped on his helmet and climbed on, I threw my arms around his waist. The vampire turned the throttle, and we sped off to my house.

When we got to my house, I went straight to my bedroom and slipped on a pair of black leather sandals. I heard my closet door (which is located right outside my bedroom) open. "Eddie, what are you doing?" I asked as I came out of my room.

"Um, I'm seeing how much room I'm going to have in here when I move in," he lied. He was hunting for my wedding dress.

"It's not here. It's at my dad's."

"Oh, come on. Why can't I see it?"

I kissed him. "You'll see it at the wedding," I replied as we headed out the door.

Fifty-seven Yetta Street is three blocks down from the Zephyr Public Library. There was barely left parking along the street, but Eddie managed to wedge the motorcycle between two television news carriages pulled by winged horses. We hopped off the bike and walked towards the brand-new Carpe Noctum building. It was a beautiful shiny brick three-story building.

David stood on the green marble steps with another Welkie by his side. This wizard was the same age as David but was a full head taller than our friend. His opal eyes scanned the crowd with confidence as he gave them a Bel-Air smile. His gray hair was parted perfectly, not a strand out of place. He smoothed down his red power tie against his three-piece black Brooks Brothers suit.

David was wearing a navy blue pinstripe suit with a white shirt and a red silk tie. But his face didn't share the same confidence as the other wizard. "Who's the guy with David?" I asked Eddie.

"Councilman Leon Laveau, I think."

"Head of the largest law firm in Zephyr?"

"And one of the most influential members of the mayor's inner circle."

"So, David must have talked to him about his financial problems," I said. "I wonder if the money problems got fixed."

Eddie nodded in agreement but said nothing. Instead, he was scanning the crowd to discover who or what was making his mentor nervous.

Councilman Laveau cleared his throat and held up his hands for silence. The crowd went still. "Ladies and gentlemen, my good friend, David Endora, has done a great thing for the vampire community across the country. Now, Zephyr has its very own Carpe Noctum," he said with a politician's smile.

A satyr reporter from one of the local television stations asked David about Carpe Noctum. The wizard cleared his throat. "Well, Cain, my brother-in-law is a vampire, and he told me how hard the life of a newly-turned vampire is. I decided to start this organization to help vampires and their families." David's speech was robotic and without passion. He took a pair of gigantic scissors and cut the blood-red ribbon tied across the front door. "The Zephyr Carpe Noctum is now opened!" he announced without passion.

Eddie and I followed David, Laveau, and the throng of spectators into the new building. I immediately noticed the royal blue marble, the beautiful, enormous UV protection picture windows, and the cathedral ceilings lined with white marble trim. Where did David get all the money for this? I mentally asked Eddie.

He shrugged as we turned a corner and walked through a long corridor lined with conference rooms. We wandered through the rest of the building for another hour listening to David talk about the uses of each room. At the end of the tour, my bladder began screaming from the cup of coffee I had picked up on the way here.

Eddie and I split up from the throng and made our way to the restrooms. Eddie waited outside while I went in. It felt like I was using the restroom of a swanky restaurant. Expensive wicker furniture, gold bathroom fixtures, and even soft cotton hand towels made one feel at home If one's home was the Ritz Carlton. After using the facilities, I ambled outside and discovered that Eddie was nowhere in sight. Maybe he needed to use the men's room. I hesitantly pushed open the door. "Eddie!" I hissed loudly.

"Shell!" Eddie poked his head from a nearby conference room.

"What are you doing in there?" I asked him as I left the restrooms and followed him to the room. It was huge with the largest oak table I had ever seen. Ten luxurious-looking black swivel chairs surrounded the table.

"I got bored."

"I wasn't in there that long!"

"Check out the chairs," the vampire said.

"And I thought you were the mature one in this relationship."

He ignored me. "They're pretty nice, and they have great features."

"Really?" I found myself inching towards one of the chairs. The force was too great, and I promptly sat down. I touched something, and the back of the chair started to vibrate. "Ooh! It massages too!"

Eddie sat in the chair next to me and pressed another button. The chair reclined back. "Nice! I could do with one of these chairs."

"We should put two of these chairs on our registry."

The vampire nodded in agreement as he clasped his hands behind his head and put his feet on the tabletop. "If you can find them for cheap."

"Really? How much are they?"

"Three thousand, I think."

I gave a low, impressive whistle. "All of this for a non-profit organization?"

Eddie opened his mouth to say David must have a very good benefactor when his heightened senses heard someone coming down the hall. "Crap! Someone's coming!" He swung his feet off the table and returned the chair to its upright position.

I frantically looked for the off switch. I found it under the seat and turned off the chair. The door started to open, and Eddie pulled me into the broom closet.

The closet was filled with brooms, mops, and buckets, along with the pleasant aroma of bleach and ammonia. There was barely enough room for both of us and therefore we were pressed together. Not that I minded, but a broom closet reeking of chemicals isn't exactly a romantic rendezvous spot with your future husband. Leave the door open, Eddie. I don't want to die of chemical asphyxiation.

He left the door open a crack, and we were thankful the two people who entered the room couldn't see us in the shadows of the broom closet.

David and Laveau stood at one end of a large oak table. Laveau was looking around the room. "David, I can see why you needed my help."

David merely nodded. "I ran into some trouble, Leon." Laveau clasped his hands behind his back as he began inspecting the room. "I suppose we weren't your first call. Most likely your last."

David opened his mouth to say something when Laveau handed him the paper. "I was very upset about this article involving your poster boy vampire."

David glanced over the paper but said nothing.

"Who is she, David?"

"Eddie's fiancée."

"But it does look bad."

"What they do is none of your business," David snapped. "Eddie would never do anything to make me look bad."

"But consider the bad press you might get."

"What are you talking about?"

"Oh, I looked into your little financial deals, and they're not quite kosher."

"Oh, and the bribes you took during your run for mayor last year were?"

A flash of anger appeared over Laveau's face but was replaced by a placating smile. "A picture can tell a thousand words."

"That picture says nothing!"

"Oh, I'm not talking about this picture. I'm talking about Diablo Island."

David gasped. "That was a long time ago."

A crocodile smile crossed Laveau's face. "And I know a young journalist who would like to get her hands on that information."

David gave a defeated sigh. "All right, Leon, you win this time. But let me warn you, if you try to exploit Eddie and his fiancée, I will not stand for it."

"Then I guess we're at a stalemate. I will show myself out." Laveau left the room, and a few minutes later, so did David.

Once the coast was clear, I shoved open the door and gasped for clean, fresh air. "I thought they would never leave." Then I got serious when I noticed Eddie was frowning. "Are you okay?"

"Something's going on with David."

"Do you know what they were talking about?"

He shook his head. "No, I don't, but I wish I did."

"I know you're worried about David, hon, but he can take care of himself. He's been around for a long time."

"You're right, babe," he said as he gave me a peck on the cheek. He glanced at his watch. "Oh, crap! I'm running late for my poker game." We left the building and hopped on the motorcycle.

Eddie asked if I wanted to go to the game, but I declined. The players consisted of my brother, Robin, Strider, Eddie's brother, Dirk, Roger Miller, a childhood friend of mine, and Tucker Tigris, our mutual friend. Tonight was the guys' night out for Eddie. He enjoyed spending time with his buddies, and I respected that.

I didn't have to worry about him gambling away money. They usually bet on candy, leftover gift certificates some of them received from work, and other non-monetary items. This time, the loser would have to wear the costume of Zephyr's baseball mascot, Billy Bob the Dragon.

The costume was old and looked like Barney the Dinosaur had sprouted wings and was beaten with an ugly stick. The last mascot had quit last year, and the coach told the team that since nobody had stepped up to the plate, one of the team players (including the manager which happened to be Roger) had to be the mascot for the first game of the season. I'd hate to be that unlucky person.

After Eddie dropped me off at my house, I realized how hungry I was. Since I am a lousy and lazy cook, I grabbed a book and my car keys and went to the nearest fast-food joint. Big Top Burger has been in business for six years, even though every food critic in the area has given it a one-third of a star rating every year. How it managed to stay in business for that long was a mystery. The circulating rumor was the owner, Larry MacElf, had some dirt on the city health inspector. The building itself was a yellow and green hole-in-the-wall that barely passed Zephyr's health inspection. The mascot was a guy who wandered around in a clown costume who must have been Pennywise's look-like with rainbow hair. Somewhere in the back of my mind, I remembered someone telling me something bad about Big Top Burger. But I was hungry, and everything else was closed.

I decided to go inside instead of going through the drive-thru. The drive-thru speaker was a giant clown who gave a creepy, maniacal, minute-long giggle before asking for your order. I certainly didn't want that image and laugh in my dreams. My dreams were disturbing enough.

After I ordered a cheeseburger, fries, and a small strawberry shake, I sat down in a nearby booth and began reading a murder mystery. Barney the Clown came over and promptly sat across from me. He leaned over and nearly shouted, "How was your meal today?" The smell of stale alcohol nearly knocked me over.

"Okay," I told him as I pressed myself into my seat.

"Are you sure?"

"Yes, it's fine."

"Would you be opposed to marrying me?"

Where did that question come from? "I'm engaged."

His face fell as if I had taken away his new puppy. He reached out and grabbed my hand. "Are you sure?" he slurred.

"Let go of my hand or I will rip your arm off and beat you with it," I calmly told him. That did the trick. The clown backed away from me.

Two booths over, I saw a couple doing things that were borderline obscene. I lost my appetite. Tossing the rest of my meal into a nearby trash bin, I grabbed my book and left the restaurant. As I headed to my car, I heard the click of a camera. I followed the noise around to the front of the restaurant, but it suddenly stopped and I found myself standing alone in the parking lot.

Chapter Five:
I Meet QT in a Burning Forest

I remembered what was so bad about Big Top Burger. My cheeseburger didn't settle with me, and I was up all night bowing before the ivory toilet god. I called in sick and slept in until early afternoon. That was when my cell phone rang to "You Sexy Thing." After I fumbled around for it, I placed it against my ear. "Eddie?"

"Shelly, did you read today's paper?"

"No, I've been sick all day."

"I'm sorry. Is there anything I can get you?"

"Actually, could you pick me up for the festival? I don't feel like driving today."

"Of course, I will. Four o'clock okay with you?"

I glanced at my bedside clock. It read one-thirty. I flopped back on my pillow. "Yeah, that sounds fine. Why did you call, hon? You mentioned the paper."

"Guess who's made front-page headlines?"

"Not us again!"

"Nope, it's the mayor!"

"Are you kidding?"

"No, apparently the mayor and an unknown female friend were getting hot and heavy at Big Top Burger last night."

"No way! I was there last night! So, that's who was sitting two booths from me."

"Why were you at Big Top Burger? The food there is nasty, and Barney the Clown is a likely sex offender."

"And an alcoholic who asks random women if they'd be opposed to marrying him."

"I sense a story, Shelly. Do tell." Once I told him the whole story, he burst out laughing. "I wish I could've seen the look on his face when you told him that. I've got to go pick up the pies from your dad, and I'll see you soon."

"See ya!" I hung up and lay in bed for another fifteen minutes. Then I dragged my bedraggled butt out of bed, brushed away the vomit taste in my mouth, showered, and got ready for the night. I threw my hair up in a wet ponytail and put on a pair of jean shorts and a red and white polka dot short-sleeved shirt before lacing up my sneakers. I gathered my paint supplies in case I needed to do some touch-ups for the banner Eddie and I had made for the diner's booth. I raided my fridge and found some French vanilla yogurt and an apple to eat while I waited for the vampire to show up.

A little after four, Eddie arrived with a bottle of pink bismuth and a steaming bowl of Dad's chicken soup. "I told your dad you weren't feeling well, and he thought you might need something to help settle your stomach before we leave." He wore beige cargo shorts, a red and blue striped polo shirt, and sneakers.

Nothing says romance like a bottle of pink bismuth. I was grateful for the medicine and took the required dosage before eating the delicious soup. "Thanks for the medicine and soup," I replied as the soup and the medicine began to ease my upset stomach. "You really know how to woo a girl, Eddie."

"It's my specialty."

We gathered my paint supplies bag and my dark green

backpack with my book sword and headed out to Eddie's carrot car. Normally, I would have thrown my purse and paint stuff in the back, but the floor and the seat were covered with four boxes filled with pies, the collapsible booth, and the rolled-up banner. I set both bags at my feet and slid into the passenger seat. "What kind of pies are in the boxes?"

Eddie got into the driver's seat, started up the engine, and inhaled the smell of the pies deeply. Even though vampires have heightened senses, Eddie did have a slight advantage. He had gotten up an hour earlier to help Dad and Amelia pack up and load everything. "Two apple, two blueberry, two apricot pecan, one grasshopper pudding, one chocolate pudding, and one strawberry cream."

I glanced at the boxes. "Save a piece of one of the pudding pies for me."

He shot me a fanged grin. "That's why I never told your dad about the cooler in the trunk. I figure that once I hand out at least one piece of both pudding pies, I'll stash them in the cooler for us later tonight."

I returned the grin. "And no one will be the wiser. Very

evil-genius of you. I like your line of thought, hon."

"Well, forty years as a vampire has made me very devious."

"Yogi Bear's got nothing on you."

The festival area is about two acres of flat green and brown ground next to ten acres of forest, known locally as Nightmare Forest. Decades ago, a mad, reclusive scientist had created about a hundred creatures that supposedly attacked and killed him. Now they are living in the darkest parts of the forest. Nobody dares, even the bravest (or stupidest) man, woman, or child, to go more than one mile into the woods for fear of being attacked by some unearthly being. Or so the urban legend goes. That doesn't stop teens with raging hormones from selecting it as a prime make-out spot or the occasional drug deal either.

About five hundred feet away from the forest entrance, restaurant owners and their employees were starting to set up their booths. Once Eddie had parked the car, I grabbed the paint supplies and the rolled-up banner while he got a tool kit and the collapsible booth. We found an empty spot, and within minutes, we had set up the booth. I took a step back and looked at the baby vomit white booth.

I glanced over at the other more appealing booths, such as green, blue, yellow, red, purple, and many more cheerful colors. "This is not an appealing color," I replied. "Where did Dad get this booth? At the discount ugly booth store?"

"Your stepmother said it was the last one available."

"Let me guess. Dad signed up late?"

"Yep!"

"At least everyone will remember the booth's color if they don't remember the pies. Okay, let's put up the banner." We unfurled the three-foot-long piece of canvas, and Eddie tacked it up on the booth with my dad's cordless nail gun.

He took a step back and looked up at the banner. That's when he began snickering.

"What's so funny?" I asked him.

"Well, people might wonder why I'm not working for your dad anymore."

"What are you talking about?" He nodded towards the banner. I joined him. "Oh, I'm such an idiot," I said as I slapped my forehead with the palm of my hand. The banner read:

Anberspn's. "I can't believe I misspelled my own last name!" I went inside the booth and grabbed my paint supplies and the little step stool that came with the booth. Snapping opening the paint tray, I began working on the letter "b" in a really pathetic attempt to repair my mistake.

Eddie stood back with his arms crossed as he watched me work. "How are you going to change a 'b' to a 'd?'"

I looked down at my paints and then at the canvas. Unfortunately, there was no eggshell white color on my tray. "Crap! How am I going to fix this?"

"Redo the whole poster?" Eddie unwisely suggested.

"No, not going to happen! I spent over an hour on this banner. I'm going to fix it." I thought about it for a minute or so, and then I had the perfect idea. I began drawing various flowers all over the signs, especially between the letters, while Eddie watched in silence. Minutes later, I stepped off the stool and joined the vampire to admire my work. "What do you think?"

"It looks like you drew flowers to cover up your spelling errors."

I narrowed my eyes at my fiancé.

He began to backpaddle. "But they're really beautiful flowers, Shelly. Shows how truly artistically talented you are." He realized he was making matters worse. "I'm going to shut up now and get the pies." Then he sprinted off to his car.

"Good thinking," I called after him. I watched him go and shook my head. He was right. My masterpiece looked completely overdone, but it looked cute.

"Well," said a sultry voice, "I guess you've screwed up even more, Shelly." I recognized that voice anywhere. Barbie Spellman looked exactly like a red-haired Barbie doll made out of hate and Botox. She wore a red mini-skirt, black blazer, red silk, button-up shirt showing off way too much cleavage, and matching go-go boots. Her digital camera was slung over one shoulder.

"Well, look what the cat dragged in!" I said with a mocking smile. "What brings you back to Zephyr? Another person's life to destroy?"

She sneered at me. "I know all about your little secret with the vampire."

"What? That Eddie and I are engaged?" The look of shock

on her face was priceless, and for once, she was speechless. I went in for the kill with a triumphant smirk on my face. "Before you start printing your tabloid trash, you might want to get all the facts first."

"So, this is the infamous Barbie Spellman," Eddie said as he noiselessly came up behind her. He stood beside me with his arms crossed. "Mind telling us why you were taking pictures of Shelly and me without our permission?"

"My responsibility to the press," Barbie said with a flick of her red hair.

"Oh, please!" I said. "You wouldn't know responsibility if it came and bit you on the butt."

Barbie smiled as she turned her camera on. "Threatening a reporter, Shelly? That's brazen of you."

Out of the corner of my eye, I saw Eddie uncross his arms as he prepared to incinerate her camera with one of his fireball spells. I slightly shook my head at him. "Take any more pictures of us without our knowledge, and I'll personally make sure your camera will never work again."

"Oh, please," Barbie said with a malicious laugh, "you two

are old news. Now I've bigger fish to fry, and there's nothing you can do about it." She slinked away.

Eddie and I were both silent for a moment, and then I spoke. "Was she talking about the photo of the mayor making out with someone other than his wife?"

"I guess so. And why should we stop her? Her photo already made the front page of the paper."

I looked at Eddie. "Because she's the Devil, and she's paranoid. And I'm pretty sure, that once again, you and I have made it onto another person's hit list."

Eddie grinned as we did a fist bump. "You know that's right, babe."

I helped him gather and arrange the pies on the booth's tabletop. Then the various aromas began to lure me away from the vampire. "I smell pretzels! Do you want me to get you one?"

"I thought you were going to help me with the booth?"

"After I get us a couple of pretzels," I said. I walked away in search of the elusive pretzel booth. Eddie called after me to remind me that he wanted mustard on his.

I finally found the pretzel booth, and as I stood in the long line, a very soft, melodious voice drifted past my ear. Apparently, I was the only one who heard the singing because everybody else was doing their own thing. The song was very catchy, and I had to find the owner of the voice.

Moving out of line, I headed towards the unkempt and possibly dangerous trail entrance to the Nightmare Forest. I fished Knowledge and a penlight out of my purse. Once I said the magic incantation, the book turned into my faithful sword in its red leather sheath. I had bought a matching leather belt for carrying my sword. I wove the belt through two slits in the top of the sheath and through the belt loops in my jeans. I began to trudge through the forest with my fighting hand on Knowledge's hilt and the other hand holding the penlight. The sun was beginning to set, and I would need the light in a few minutes.

I navigated through the fallen branches and the roots until I came to a small clearing surrounded by rock trees. These magical plants are made completely from rocks, but they grow like trees. Sitting on one of the four-inch thick, concrete branches was a wild griffin preening himself and singing "Love is Knocking at my Door." It had a golden eagle head, matching eight-foot-long wings, sharp talons, and the tawny back end of a lion. I should have been terrified, but since griffins don't talk, much less sing, I was curious. "You can sing?" I asked it.

The griffin stopped singing at the sound of my voice and gave a shout of surprise. It tumbled off its perch and landed on the ground, not on its feet, but on its side. "Where did you come from?" it asked in a male voice.

"Griffins can't talk! You're a robot or something, right?"

He scrambled to his feet and combed back his crest of feathers with one of his talons. "No one can imitate the great voice of QT."

I let out a bark of laughter. "You're that famous singer who disappeared sixteen years ago? You're pulling my leg, right? Am I on Candid Camera?"

The griffin snorted disdainfully. "I am most certainly not. I am Quentin Tamself, but you can call me Quentin."

"My name's Shelly Anderson. But you're not an elf."

"Well, I would be if my ex hadn't turned me into a griffin. It was over a little misunderstanding."

"Ooh, I sense a story." I sat down on a fallen log. "Do tell, if you don't mind."

The griffin gave an exaggerated sigh. "Fine! Sixteen years ago, my fiancée, Ruby Medea, out of anger turned me into a griffin."

Turning someone into a non-talking animal borders on dark magic, and Welkies use the animalize spell when they are angry. "What did you do to tick her off?"

Quentin shrugged. "It was just a misunderstanding about her best friend and me. She told me I could spend the rest of my life crooning to other griffins."

"Ouch!" I said. Wild male griffins are notorious for having two or three mates at a time. Oh, the irony! "So, she turned you into a griffin, huh?"

"And I certainly couldn't go out on stage as a griffin!"

"So, what happened to your ex?"

"Well, she teleported somewhere, and I have been trying to track her down for the past sixteen years so she can turn me back to my former glory." Quentin smiled the best a griffin could. "But I have finally found her. She's here in Zephyr under the name of Barbie Spellman."

"No way!"

"Do you know her?"

"The parasitic creature of the free press? Yeah, I know her, and believe me, Quentin, she will exploit you to no end. She has no soul."

Quentin looked shocked. "That's not true!"

"Denial is not just a river," I muttered under my breath. Suddenly, I was aware of a whistling noise above my head. I looked up to see a saucer-shaped object the size of a grand piano come barreling down from the sky with thick black smoke trailing behind it. It was heading straight for us!

Quentin moved much faster than I did. "Get on my back!" he yelled as he ran towards me, wings ready for flight.

Not hesitating at all, I leaped on his back and wrapped my arms around his feathered neck. Within seconds, we were flying up into the night sky. BOOM! A huge flash of light penetrated the dark forest when the object hit the ground right where I had been standing a few seconds earlier. Quentin lost control. He began plummeting towards the rock trees.

"Pull up! Pull up!" I shouted as I tugged hard on his

feathers.

"Good God, woman! That hurt!" Quentin shouted as he snapped from his stupor. He began soaring higher and higher as flames raced across the forest floor.

Festival goers began screaming and running towards the blaze. Not surprisingly, Barbie was leading the pack. Behind her was the Zephyr Fire Department, which consisted of a wizard who specialized in creating storms, two Winged Ones, and three centaurs.

"Okay, let's get out of here," I said to Quentin. I turned Knowledge back into a book and put it into my purse.

"Where can I take you?" Quentin asked.

"Eddie's probably flipping out right now. I have to find him." I searched the fairgrounds and quickly spotted the butt-ugly booth. "There!" I showed Quentin. "My fiancé is inside that booth."

"Got it!" He began to beat his wings faster and faster as we headed towards the ground. He overestimated his landing, and to my horror, we began rapidly skidding toward the booth. Actually, it was the back of the booth, but at this point, technicalities didn't matter.

"Quentin, slow down!" I screamed as I saw Eddie. I could see tomorrow's headlines: Vampire Killed in Pie Booth Accident. Police Suspect Girlfriend Error.

The vampire looked up in shock to see Quentin and me come careening toward him at an incredibly vicious speed. "What the?" he yelled.

I let go of Quentin's neck and waved my arms frantically as I screamed, "Eddie, get out of the way! Get out of the way!" Not wasting another breath, my fiancé dropped to the ground and rolled out of the danger zone. A very smart move on his part, because a moment later, Quentin screeched to a stop/crash. The back of the booth cracked in half horizontally when the griffin hit it with his side. I fell off and landed in a disarray of pie and scattered pieces of booth. The banner had been torn in half and floated gently down on top of me.

Squeezing my eyes shut, I lay there for a few painful moments until I heard Eddie running towards me. "Shelly, are you okay?" he asked as he pulled the banner off me.

I managed a nod. "I think so," I replied as I grabbed his

hand and pulled myself up. Something wet and squishy was on the seat of my pants. "Please, tell me I was sitting in pie!"

Eddie didn't object to inspecting my butt. "I think it's apricot pecan. Or maybe apple."

Quentin was eating what looked like chocolate pudding pie. He looked up at us. "Shelly, I should have told you. I have trouble landing."

"You've been a griffin for sixteen years, and you have trouble landing?" I said as I walked from the mess with Eddie by my side.

"Oh, come on, can't you give a guy a break?" Quentin asked.

"What was your intended goal? Landing or death? Because I think we came fairly close to the latter."

Eddie realized I was arguing with a griffin. He made a time-out gesture with his hands. "Hold it! Hold it!" he said. He looked at Quentin with his green eyes. "You can talk?"

"Yeah!" Quentin replied as if that explained everything.

I decided to clear things up for the vampire. "Quentin is an enchanted griffin."

Eddie regarded us quizzically. "Right!"

My head ached. "Okay, let me give you the Reader's Digest Condensed version," I told the whole story in less than a minute. "So, Quentin thinks that Barbie will turn him back."

Eddie began laughing. "Right, she'll take you back after she exploits your story as the greatest sex scandal of all time, and then spit you out like a piece of tobacco."

Quentin shook his head in disbelief. "Ruby is many things, but she is not a man-eater."

"Have you ever read any of her articles?" I asked.

"No, but—."

"She is not a nice person," Eddie explained.

"Well, what am I going to do? She has to turn me back so that I can go on a comeback tour."

"Okay!" I said. Quentin's music wasn't exactly Grammy-quality, but it wasn't too bad either. He had a good singing voice, and according to the internet, he had made only one album. But he seemed to be a nice, misguided griffin. "You need someplace to crash? Figuratively, of course." I ran my fingers through my hair and discovered the remains of grasshopper pudding pie. Yuck.

"Sure!" Quentin said.

"I've got an empty stable you can stay in as long as you want."

"Shell," Eddie said as he looked at me, "I think I might have a couple of old blankets in the trunk of my car. You can sit on them." He looked around the festival grounds. Not a soul was in sight. It looked like the party was over at the forest fire. "What's up with the fire?"

"Some kind of alien spaceship came out of nowhere, and would have killed me had it not been for Quentin here."

Eddie gave the griffin an impressive nod. "Thank you, Quentin, but really, work on your landing!" He surveyed the damage to the booth. "How am I going to explain this to your father?"

I thought for a moment. "Stampede of crazy festival goers?"

Eddie shook his head as he brushed strawberry cream pie debris off my shoulder. "I don't think your dad's going to buy that one."

"What about a death ray from an alien spaceship?" I suggested.

"Aliens don't exist."

"Seriously?"

Eddie nodded.

"This is a land of magic and myth, and yet there's no such thing as aliens?"

"None that we've discovered," Eddie replied. "Why don't we just tell your dad the truth?"

"Do you really want Barbie Spellman to expose Quentin here? I know Dad and Amelia would never tell, but someone else might get wind that QT is an enchanted griffin and tell the press."

"Plus, Ruby used her own variation of an animalize spell," Quentin added.

"What does that mean?" I asked.

"Only she can recant the spell," Eddie said. "I don't think that she will ever turn him back. She might make him mute."

Quentin gasped. "She would do that?"

Eddie and I looked at the griffin in surprise. "How long have you known Ruby?" Eddie asked.

"We dated for about a month before we were engaged, and about two weeks before she turned me into a griffin," Quentin replied.

"Okay," I said, "Quentin, you can still stay at my place and try to find Ruby/Barbie." I had given up trying to convince the griffin that his ex was a soulless witch. I picked up my purse and glanced down at the pieces of pie dripping from my clothes. "Honey," I said to Eddie, "can you take me home? Quentin can follow us."

Chapter Six:
Take Me Out at the Ballgame

My alarm went off at the ungodly hour of sixty-thirty the next morning. My body still ached from the crash, and after I had showered and got ready for work, I downed some ibuprofen. Drinking my first cup of coffee and eating my bagel, I noticed something in my backyard. "What the?" I asked. Then I realized what I was looking at. I threw open the sliding door. "Quentin!"

The griffin appeared from behind the red and white stable. "What?" he asked.

I pointed to the brown and red object lying in the tall grass. "Care to explain the deer carcass in my backyard?"

"Breakfast!"

I swallowed hard trying not to have my breakfast up in my throat to join his breakfast. "Okay," I said to him after I regained my strength, "if you're going to stay with me, there needs to be some ground rules. Rule number 1: Carcasses of any kind will not be left in my backyard. They will be eaten where you found them. Rule number 2: You have to act like a domesticated griffin."

"What do you mean by that?"

"I'll be getting out of work around five, and then you are going to get fitted for a saddle and a bridle."

"No way! I'm a free, flying griffin."

"No, the last thing I need is my place crawling with the media because someone found out that I have a wild, talking griffin staying with me."

"How about I give you a ride to work?"

"No, thank you," I said quickly. "I'll walk." I shuddered at the thought of the griffin leveling the first floor of the Zephyr Public Library. "Just keep a low profile until I get back."

Once I got to work, the entire staff was abuzz about what had happened at the Taste of Zephyr. From gathering bits and pieces, I finally surmised what was going on. The headlines shouted out: Aliens in Our Mist? According to Fiona Littlehorn, the object that crashed into the woods was a spaceship, and perhaps little green men were running around loose in Zephyr. Aliens don't exist, do they? In your face, Eddie!

The rest of the day was pretty busy. It seemed like every single patron was checking out books on UFOs and aliens. I wanted to get some information on aliens, but instead, I checked out a few books on griffin riding. I had never ridden a griffin until last night, and according to the books, the saddle for a griffin was only one size bigger than a winged horse's.

After I got out of work, I took Quentin to Jack's Saddle and Tack Shoppe. Looking at riding materials is one thing, but getting an overly chatty griffin to wear them is a different matter altogether. When Eddie asked me about it later, I told him it was like "dressing a two-year-old, but worse." One very long hour later, we left the store equipped with a saddle, bit, bridle, reins, and a special griffin calling whistle I wore as a necklace around my neck. Off we headed to the baseball field to watch the first game of the Dragons.

When we got to the parking lot of the brand-spanking new Silenus Stadium, I tied Quentin's reins to a wrought iron fence. "You should let me roam around," he suggested.

I looked at him. "Why? Are the reins still too tight for you?"

"Like I said, I'm a free griffin."

"You're going to be a dead one if you don't stop whining and act normal. I'll be out to check on you at halftime."

I began walking to the ticket counter when I noticed David arguing with a middle-aged fairy with a graying buzz cut and a crisp black suit. One of the fairy's army-style camouflaged wings had been torn up, a black eye patch covered the scar over his right eye, and both of his feather antennae were missing. I finally realized who he was.

It was Rufus Mothman, a retired, five-star general who was a decorated Wixom War hero and now fought political battles as one of the mayor's councilmen. Standing next to the General was a muscular, stout man with no neck, dressed in all black. Even his eyes were black. He acted like his bodyguard, but I didn't understand why the war hero would need someone to protect him.

"The papers are saying a UFO caused the fire, but you know what it really was, don't you," David said to the General.

"I don't know what you're talking about, Endora."

"We aren't at war anymore, Mothman. Someone could have been killed."

"You don't know what's at stake!"

"Lives were at stake last night."

"As at Diablo Island."

"You don't know what really happened there."

The thug balled up his fists and moved towards David, but the General held him back. "No, Xerox!" He looked at the wizard. "Let's forget this conversation ever happened, Endora." That was when they noticed me. The General put an arm around David's shoulders who reluctantly accepted it, and they all walked into the stadium.

When I got to the ticket counter, Billy Bob the Dragon had a cloth bag over his shoulder and was selling brightly colored giant foam fingers advertising that the Dragons were number one. "Go, Dragons, go," the mascot said in a bored voice. "Support the Dragons."

"Roger?" I asked him.

The mascot took off his removable head, and my childhood friend, Roger Miller, an assistant district attorney, glared at me with his bright green eyes. "What do you want, Shelly?"

I pulled my camera from my purse. "Permission to send this Kodak moment to your girlfriend?"

"You do, and I'll kill you. Then I'll use my molekineis to reconstruct you and kill you again."

I laughed at the red-haired, former college linebacker. "Good luck with that, Roger. I can kick your butt any day of the week."

He nodded. "From what Eddie has told me, you're probably right."

"Don't worry. I won't take any pictures of you in that ugly getup."

"It smells like feet and wet dog. I think Eddie cheated the other night. Did you know that he was the first one to fold, and we were only five minutes into the game?"

I chuckled. "Sounds like something he would do. He did not want to be the one wearing that. Are your dad and Libby here?"

"No, Dad's working Eddie's shift, and Libby's helping him out."

I remembered the conversation with the General and David. "Do you know what happened at the Taste of Zephyr?"

"The papers said a UFO caused the fire."

"I thought you might have some more information, you being the assistant DA and all."

"Ask Robin. He's heading up the case. He might cheat, though," Roger added bitterly.

I smiled. "He folded too?"

"Two minutes after Eddie."

I smiled. "That's my brother for you. See you later, Roger." I waved goodbye. "Go, Dragons!"

"Shut up," he said as he put his costume head back on.

After I bought my ticket, I made my way to Dad and Amelia who were saving a seat for me on the bleachers. The perfectly cut grass of the baseball diamond was bathed in the white stadium lights. I scanned the field for my fiancé when I remembered he played center field for the Dragons, an amateur league baseball team consisting of a vampire, a werewolf, a weretiger, two satyrs, a centaur, a fairy, a Winged One, and a regular human. With baseball, there is a definite "no magic" rule. Even in this magical city, baseball is a favorite pastime.

I took out my camera from my purse and began to take pictures of the team as they warmed up. My brother, Robin, had called me the night before to see if I could take some pictures of the game. His girlfriend couldn't make it, and he wanted to send her a few pictures of him throwing the winning pitch.

Someone was tapping my shoulder. "Shelly, I think that Brooke wanted pictures of Robin, not Eddie."

I glanced over at Dad, who was sitting next to me. "Sorry," I said as I gave a sheepish grin.

"Oh, Timothy," my stepmother playfully scolded, "let Shelly take pictures of her fiancé." She put an arm around my dad's waist.

"Thank you, Amelia," I said. "Here, Dad," I said, turning towards them. "Just to make you feel better, I'll take a picture of you two." I focused the camera and took a picture of the very happy couple.

"Play ball!" the umpire shouted. And the game commenced. The Muses, an all-girl team, was up to bat with an elf reporter named Fiona Littlehorn. I thought this was very ironic because her husband, a satyr detective, was the third baseman for the Dragons. She hit the ball with a great WHACK and sent it flying towards center field.

Eddie had his striking green eyes concentrating on the ball the second it left my brother's hand. He began running backward as the baseball flew above him. Just when I thought that he was going to collide with the wall, he leaped about a foot off the ground and attempted a mid-air catch. The ball flew inches above his catcher's mitt, bounced off the wall, and rolled a few feet away from him. He retrieved the ball and tossed it to second base where the elf was rounding the corner. Tucker Tigris, a weretiger, caught the ball but dropped it almost immediately. No score for the Dragons.

By the time the fifth inning started, the score was 3 to 1, not in our favor. I shook my head in desperation. Normally, the Dragons are a great team, but this game was going horribly. I mentioned this to my dad.

"The team's probably getting used to playing on a new field," Dad replied as he watched Robin pitch a no-hitter to the opposing team's batter. "All right, son!" he shouted as my brother struck her out.

"Dad," I asked as soon as I took another picture of Robin striking out the batter for a second time, "when did the city get the field?"

"I think it was last fall, Shelly. General Rufus Mothman had given it to the city. Why do you ask?"

"Just curious," I said as I snapped another picture of the game. I flagged down the elf selling stadium food and bought myself a box of popcorn and some bottled water.

"So, Shelly, I heard that there was a little incident with my booth at the festival," Dad said.

Eddie, you couldn't just lie, could you? "Yeah, I've been having trouble training the griffin I just got," I said. Okay, not a complete lie. "I'll pay for the damages, Dad."

"You weren't hurt, were you?" Amelia asked me.

"Nothing that ibuprofen and rest couldn't fix."

"How's the griffin ride?" Dad asked.

"He's getting better." Didn't crash into the parking lot, I added to myself.

"His name?"

"Quentin. I got him from a seller online." Complete lie right there. I wasn't sure how long I could keep up the charade. I looked out to the field as a quick distraction. "Oh, look! The Dragons are up to bat!"

I have to admit this was my favorite part of the game because the Dragons called up their best batter. Eddie stepped up to home plate and he took a couple of practice swings, mainly to impress me. It was working. Swing, batta, batta.

The enchantress tipped her baseball cap forward and pitched a fast curveball toward the vampire.

The ball hit the bat with a loud WHACK as Eddie sent it soaring into the air. He dropped the bat and began booking around the bases at full speed, which is about as fast as a racing greyhound.

"Come on, Eddie!" I shouted, cupping my hands to my mouth. "You can make it!" I watched as the Muse's left fielder tossed the ball to the second baseman who in turn threw it towards home plate. Which was exactly where my boyfriend was

heading. When the vampire slid into the home plate, the umpire,

a tall minotaur by the name of Cox, yelled, "Safe!"

Which was the most illogical thing to say because a loud

BOOM accompanied by a bright flash of light rocked the

stadium. Seconds later, something huge and purple was

hovering up in the sky. It was about the length and height of two

school buses with wings twice its size. It was covered in purple

scales except for a long pink stripe running along its underbelly.

It had one deadly-looking, long horn protruding from its

football-shaped head. Right below the horn was one huge,

Buick-size eye. An oval-shaped mouth was filled with row upon

row of sharp teeth.

It hovered over the crowd, scanning us with its deep

purple eye. Finally, the thing's eye settled on David. The wizard

shook his head in horror. "No!" he shouted. Nothing happened

for a few terrifying seconds, and then the creature darted away

from David and stared down at the mayor and his wife. Then a

blast of neon blue light erupted from its mouth, nearly blinding us

all. Screams came from the crowd, and I shut my eyes tight as I used my arm as a shield.

When I opened my eyes seconds later, the creature was gone, but Eddie was by my side. "You all right, Shelly?" he asked.

"I-Um-I'm fine. What happened?" I asked. Then a powerful, acrid smell sucker-punched my olfactory senses. "What is that smell?" I shielded my nose with my hand.

Eddie did the same thing with his nose. "Burning flesh! That thing torched the mayor and his wife!"

Chapter Seven:
Meanwhile Back at the Haunted Fort. . .

After the horrific event at the game last night, the city called for a day of mourning and closed down all municipal offices, including the library. The day was absolutely beautiful, and I was sitting outside on the plastic wicker furniture on my patio with my tabletop easel and my laptop. Quentin was sitting on the lawn, preening his wings.

I was trying to recall what the creature looked like by drawing it. The papers were saying that a strange alien was responsible for killing the mayor and his wife, but that didn't make sense. Why attack just them? A wild, dangerous animal, no matter what planet it comes from, doesn't attack one or two people and then just disappear. The mayor and his wife definitely were targeted, but by whom and why? I couldn't figure it out.

Once I finished the final draft of what I remembered what

the creature had looked like, I tried researching it on the net while humming a few bars of Sheb Wooley's famous song. I discovered absolutely nothing. "Hey, Quentin!" I said, my eyes still on the computer screen.

"Yeah?" The griffin stopped preening himself and looked up.

I held up the open sketchbook. "Have you ever seen this creature flying around?"

"Yeah, I saw one hanging around Diablo Island when I was hunting for my lunch."

Diablo Island. There was that place again. Almost every conversation with David had consisted of some mention of this place. "Where's Diablo Island?"

Quentin shuddered. "About six miles from the docks of the Sapphire Sea."

"What's wrong?"

"When I flew over the island, some strange things were going on down there."

I gave him a puzzled look. "Like what?"

"Weird lights and noises were coming from the

abandoned fort, and there was this smell.”

“Smell?”

“Yeah, like a sweet, sticky smell.”

“Really?” I was intrigued. “Can you take me over there?”

“Why? That place is probably haunted!”

“Oh, come on! Where’s your sense of adventure?” Quentin began backing up. “No way! That island’s cursed or something.”

I did an eye roll. “This coming from an enchanted griffin? Come on, it’ll be fun!” The griffin shook his head violently. “Look, I’ll even let you bring your supper here for a late-night snack. Just for one night only, of course.”

“All right! Let’s do it!” Typical guy. Will do anything for food. It took us about fifteen minutes to get ready because Quentin said that his saddle gave him a rash, and he really should have a blanket under it. Armed with my sword, cell phone, and camera in a backpack, I hoisted myself up onto Quentin’s back. “Let’s ride!”

The flight over the Sapphire Sea had turned quite cold. I

was glad I wore a light hoodie but had not been smart enough to bring gloves. The icy, cold winds nearly whipped me off Quentin, and I had to hold tightly on the reins with my frozen hands. We finally landed on the browned grass next to the granite entrance of an old, abandoned fort surrounded by a twenty-five-foot tall stone wall. There were three buildings taller than the wall and looked like they were all connected by various tunnels.

"Stay here, and be on the lookout for anything suspicious," I ordered Quentin. A sweet, sickly smell permeated the air, making me gag slightly. It took me a few minutes to locate the scent coming from the entrance of the biggest building. Taking my flashlight out of my bag, I shone it down a seemingly endless flight of stone stairs. "Quentin!" I shouted. "I'm going down this tunnel!" I carefully edged my way down the steep stairs moistened by the sea salt air.

The beam fell on some strange symbols lining the wall. Some were recent, some old. I wanted to take pictures of them but was unsure of how well they would show up. Grabbing a receipt from my bag, I did some very crude sketches on the back.

As soon as I put away my artwork, two things happened. First, a low foghorn-like sound came from the darkness at the bottom of the stairs. I turned around and headed up the stairs. The last thing I wanted was to slip and fall with nobody to help me. A shadowy figure ran in front of the entrance. "Hello!" I called. "Who's there!"

By the time I reached the top of the stairs, the person darted into the entrance of the building to the left. I managed to get a fleeting glimpse of the person, but I couldn't believe my eyes. What was David doing here? "David!" I yelled to the wizard. "It's me, Shelly!"

No answer. I looked up to see the sky go from clear and sunny to dark and extremely windy. I tried calling for Quentin, but the winds drowned out my voice. Finally, the ominous clouds broke loose in a torrent of rain. I blew on the whistle that hung around my neck, and seconds later, the griffin was landing by my side.

"Come on! Let's go!" he shouted over the wind and rain. "If this gets any worse, I don't think I can fly in this weather!"

I nodded as I pulled up my hood. Throwing on my

backpack, I scrambled on Quentin's back. Talk about major turbulence! The winds got stronger as we were tossed about in the air, but the griffin managed to fly out of the storm, and I managed not to get motion sickness. Once we cleared the island, the day was bright and sunny. I still could hear the pounding of the rain, and so I glanced over my shoulder. The storm was centered on the island only. "That's weird!" I said.

"What?" Quentin asked.

"The storm. It's only surrounding the island," I said as I pulled out my camera and took a few pictures.

"It's probably just an isolated storm."

"Or someone could have caused it." Like David. But why would he create a storm? He was the only other person at the fort. Furthermore, what was he doing there to begin with? And what was that noise that came from the bottom of the stairs? This would mean some hardcore research on my part.

As soon as I got home, I let Quentin go hunting, and I changed into dry clothes. Then I sat down at my computer and did some web research. First, I decided to learn more about

Diablo Island. According to an article on the online encyclopedia, Knowledge Wizard.com, Diablo Island was an armory operated by both civilians and military personnel during the Wixom War. It had been abandoned since what the public called Diablo's Tragedy with only a handful of survivors. There were rumors that black magic had destroyed the Wixom warships. I tried to find out who the survivors were, but nothing turned up.

The next thing I tried was investigating the symbols I had drawn. I pulled a soggy piece of paper out of my bag. "Oh, crap!" I said as I tried to make out the ink-drawn symbols that were now running down the paper. Note to self: Get a notebook with a waterproof cover. Shutting my eyes, I tried to recreate the symbols in my mind. But when I drew them on my sketch pad, they looked nothing like what I had seen. The web yielded no results. "Eddie might know what they are." I debated on waking up the vampire just to ask what the symbols were and then decided against it. I was going to see him tomorrow night anyway.

My cell phone vibrated. I remembered I had turned it off and had forgotten to check my messages "Hello?"

"Shelly, I've been trying to get a hold of you all day," my best friend from childhood, Lisa Miller, said to me.

"Sorry, I had turned off my phone."

"I've got some great news!"

"What!"

"I can't tell you over the phone. You want to meet for dinner at the Groovy Vegetable at six."

"Sure. See you there." I hung up and went back to my computer. After a couple of hours of fruitless research, I decided to watch the 5 o'clock news before meeting Lisa at the Groovy Vegetable. The biggest news was that the announcement the mayor and his wife's funerals were going to be held the next morning at eleven. Authorities still had no idea what happened on the ball field, other than the fact the Dragons were spanked in their first game.

Then two commentators talked about who would be the likely candidates to fill the mayoral seat. It was at this point I shut off the television. I wasn't into politics back in my world, and I'm definitely not into politics here in Zephyr. There are two main political parties here in Zephyr, the Lincolnites and Jeffersonians.

The Lincolnite party favors limited government in our nation whereas the Jeffersonian party supports a larger government oversight. On paper, both Eddie and I are Jeffersonians, but we don't always agree with either the parties' politics.

Lisa was running fifteen minutes late when she got to the Groovy Vegetable restaurant. The twenty-something wedding planner was wearing a navy blue pantsuit and matching pumps. Her long, platinum blond hair was in a double French braid. "Shelly," she said shaking her head at my jeans, button-up red shirt, and sneakers which were emitting a slight, funky smell, "we're at dinner."

I ignored her comment about my clothing as I stole a glance around the closet-size, seat-yourself diner. It looked like the love child of a flower child's VW van and a health food store. Incense candles wafted throughout the diner which was painted tie-dyed. I was beginning to feel like I was living in a yellow submarine. The lighting was so low I could barely read the menu. I pulled out my penlight from my purse and read the eco-friendly menu.

The food was pretty good. I ordered spaghetti and homemade marinara sauce with garlic bread. Lisa ordered eggplant lasagna with a side salad.

"So," I asked once the waiter had left, "what's up?"

`"Haven't you noticed?" Lisa asked waving the gigantic diamond ring on her finger. "Dirk asked me to marry him last night!"

"Congratulations! So, tell me everything!"

"He took me to Ambrosia, and on the second course, he got down on one knee, pulled out the ring, and asked me to marry him! It was so romantic!"

"That's awesome! Just think, soon we'll be family!"

"Our kids will grow up together, and—." She paused and sniffed the air. "What's that smell?"

The smell I had encountered earlier was getting funkier and funkier. Then I realized it was coming from my shoe. I glanced down and noticed a small, glowing glob on the outside of my left shoe. When I removed it with my napkin, it left a burn the size of a cigarette and proceeded to burn through the hemp napkin. I quickly dropped the charred napkin and the glob into my water glass. It bubbled rapidly for a second or two and then fizzled out.

Lisa's green eyes were round with shock. "What did you step in, Shelly?"

I, who was equally shocked, shook my head. "I have no idea, but I know someone who does. Want to get out of here and go see Professor Faraday?" Professor Faraday Silver is a science professor at the local university. This centaur has the IQ of Stephen Hawkins and the hours of both the living and the undead. I swear, this guy must never sleep. He is a consultant with the Zephyr police and a good friend of my dad's.

The laboratory of the centaur, Faraday Silver, was on the west side of Zephyr University. It was a small, one-room building that I hated going into because of all of the pungent smells that were always in the air, and I felt like I was back in high school science class. Lisa opted to stay in my car, while I went in through the double steel doors, a safety precaution in case one of Faraday's experiments went awry. I walked up to one of the high lab tables.

A centaur in his late fifties was holding up a purple flask of foaming liquid with one of his gloved, human-like hands. A lab coat coated with various stains covered the man part of the half-man, half-horse creature. Green plastic goggles protected his black eyes. His head was completely bald. "Ah, Miss Anderson, I understand congratulations are in order," he said without looking up from the flask.

"What for?" I asked.

"Your engagement to Eddie Van Helsing. Your father told me the other day when I came into his dining establishment." He handed me an extra pair of goggles. "Put these on, stand back, and cover your ears."

Doing what I was told, I took two giant steps backward and plugged my fingers into my ears. Moments later, there was a slight BOOM, and the foam shot up into the air and splattered the entire ceiling in purple goo. It was an improvement to the puke-green color that had occupied the ceiling. I suspected in another time and dimension the ceiling had once been white.

He pushed his goggles to the top of his head and looked up. "Fascinating. Can travel upwards at incredible speeds, but completely indestructible." He put the flask on a Bunsen burner. "What can I do for you?"

I put the blob that was still sticking to the charred napkin on the table. "This was sticking to my shoe. Could you do some tests on it and tell me what it is?" I decided not to tell him that I found it while exploring an abandoned island.

He gave me a huge smile as if I had given him a million dollars to fund the next moon landing. "I will accomplish this task posthaste! It may take a day or two for the results."

"That's no problem," I replied as I began fishing through my purse for a pen and something to write on, "Let me give you my cell phone number." I jotted it down and handed the paper to the centaur.

That night around eight o'clock, I sat on my couch and called Eddie. "Whatcha up to?" I asked.

"Outside the diner eating the primavera I made last night and avoiding the political tension inside," the vampire answered.

"What political tension?"

"You didn't hear?"

"Hear what?"

"Two people have announced their candidacy for the mayoral seat!"

"Really? That's quick!"

I heard Eddie take a bite of his food before responding. "I know. It's like they haven't even closed the lid on the mayor's coffin."

"Ooh, the vampire makes a pun about a coffin. You're funny, Eddie!"

"I try. Anyway, guess who is running for office."

I shrugged. "I don't know. Who?"

"Councilman Laveau and Councilman Mothman."

"No way! Why would anyone want to vote for them? They're both corrupt politicians. Last election they had been accused of taking bribes."

"But conveniently there was no evidence."

"True, but unfortunately we're stuck with them."

"You know what's going to happen. There will be political debates all over Zephyr."

"Oh, that's already started here at the diner."

I groaned. "It's not Dad and Bruce, is it?"

"Yep. Mr. Miller likes Laveau because he's a Jeffersonian, and your dad likes Mothman because he's a Lincolnite. Then they got into a heated debate without really listening to each other's ideas. Then they asked me who I thought the better candidate was."

"What was your response?"

"I told them I don't like politics at all. I went through enough of that crap when I was with the Agency."

"That's the problem with politics," I said. "Both sides could care less about each other's ideas. Instead of coming to a workable compromise between parties, they fight like kids at recess. Nothing gets done because they aren't listening to their constituents. If I were a world leader, I would be a neutral party and listen to what the people want, not what the politicians want." I paused. "I'm stepping off my soapbox."

"Wow!" I heard the impressiveness in Eddie's voice. "You should run for office. You'd be great at it."

"Nah, I'm not cut out for that. No one would listen to me."

"I would, and I'm not saying that because you're my

fiancée. That's the smartest thing I've heard all day."

I smiled. "Thank you. So how did you get out of the heated debate between Dad and Bruce?"

"I may have used some of my stealth spy moves when leaving the diner."

"What?" I asked with a smile. "You ran out the back door?"

"Slipped, babe, I slipped out the back door."

I laughed. Then I became serious as I remembered what I had found out today. "What do you know about Diablo Island?"

"Not much. Just what they reported in the papers at the time. Why do you ask?"

"Almost every time I see David talking to someone, Diablo Island is always brought up. He got really upset when both Laveau and Mothman had mentioned it."

"That's weird."

"You think that's weird. Guess what I found out today."

"What?"

I told him what happened at Diablo Island. "Why was David there?"

"Are you sure it was David?"

“I’m positive.”

“Then I have no idea.”

“All right, then what do you think those symbols are?”

“Don’t know off-hand, but I’ll look them up when I get home tonight. Look, my lunch is almost over, and I’ll call you later.”

“All right,” I said with a smile. “Love you, Eddie.”

“Love you too, Shelly. Good night, babe.”

“Good night, hon.” I hung up my phone and headed off to bed. But I didn’t get to sleep until a few hours later because my head was filled with the strange things I had learned today, and nothing seemed to make sense.

Chapter Eight:
David is Rushed to the ER

The next day at work, everyone was taking very fervent political sides. The vehement discussions in the lunch room practically heated the food without using the microwaves. Except for me. I took the side of popping in the headphones to my mp3 player that Dad and Amelia gave me for Christmas and read some bridal books for ideas for the wedding. It was a great plan that was held throughout the day.

Around six-thirty that night, Eddie knocked on my front door. I let him in and nodded my approval at his royal blue long-sleeve shirt, black jeans, and black boots. I had changed into my short jean skirt, a green and white striped shirt with three-quarter length sleeves, and brown flats. We were going over to David's on Eddie's lunch break to ask the wizard about officiating at our wedding.

"You look as lovely as ever, Shelly," Eddie said as we kissed.

"You're looking handsome yourself," I replied.

The vampire broke off the kiss as he sniffed the breeze was coming in from an open window. "Why is there a deer carcass in your backyard?"

I threw open the sliding door. Eddie was right. A gutted deer was sprawled in front of my sliding door. "Quentin!" I shouted.

No answer. The dumb griffin was probably out hunting. "I feel like I'm dealing with a two-year-old. He knows that I don't want him leaving his leftovers all over the place. It's disgusting!"

"He's a griffin, Shelly."

"Yes, but would you leave rotten carcasses all over if you were a talking griffin?"

The vampire looked shocked I would even suggest something like that. "I can't drink blood, and even if I could, all the empty blood bottles would quickly be put in the recycling bin right before you came over," he said with a grin. "I wouldn't worry about it, babe. You can hunt him down when we get back."

"Okay," I said as I closed the sliding door. I grabbed my purse, along with a notebook and pen, off of my kitchen table.

"What's the notebook for?" Eddie asked as we headed out the door.

"I wrote down possible food ideas for the reception. I thought we could talk about them on the way over to David's."

"Sounds good to me," Eddie said. "I'm always up to talking about food." We walked to his carrot car, and he opened the passenger door for me. We both got in, and he started up the car. "What's on the menu?"

I glanced at my notes. "Well, I was considering meals, but then I realized if the reception was going to be around eight-thirty at night, then we should just serve finger foods."

"Great idea! Most people will have eaten dinner before the ceremony anyway, but we should probably state on the invitation we're going to be serving finger foods."

I raised an eyebrow. "You want the invitation saying 'Finger foods and dessert to follow ceremony?' I want the guests to think we're classy, yet deceptively cheap. No, we'll put hors

d'oeuvres on the invite."

Eddie shrugged. "Fine with me, but we need to taste our

options." He pulled into the driveway of the two-story colonial. He

became dead serious the moment he noticed the door wide

open. Without saying a word, he quickly parked the car and ran

to the front door, with me closely following. "David!" he called

with a hint of panic in his voice.

By the time I had reached the door, Eddie was already

inside. The strong, copper scent of blood filled the air. I skidded

to a stop, nearly slipping on the bright red blood coating the hall's

wooden floor. My heart caught in my throat at the scene in front

of me.

Eddie was kneeling beside the wizard who was bleeding

profusely from various gaping wounds in the chest and

abdomen. Blood flowed from a huge gash on his forehead. David

was slipping in and out of consciousness. The vampire peeled

off his shirt and began tearing it into bandages. There was too

much blood and not enough shirt to cover the wounds. He was

checking David's breathing and barely looked up at me. "Shelly, call 911!"

Both my mind and body froze in horror at the scene. I barely registered what Eddie had told me to do. I had never seen that much blood in my life. I shut my eyes as the dream I had of David covered in blood converged onto this horrible scene

"Shelly!" Eddie shouted at me, an angry edge to his voice. "Call 911 now!"

I fumbled for my cell phone. My shaking hands dropped it on the floor. A wave of nausea and dizziness swept over me as I fell to my knees. I shut my eyes again.

Eddie picked up my cell phone, and I heard him call for an ambulance. Shelly, why don't you go outside and get some air? he immediately suggested. I've got this.

I managed a nod and weakly got to my feet. Stumbling outside, I could hear my fiancé say, "Come on, David. Stay with me. Help is on the way."

The drive to the hospital was silent. Eddie's bloodstained hands were gripping the steering wheel so hard I thought it would break off. I sat next to him staring at the side mirror at the circus outside David's house. Detectives and crime scene investigators ducked under the crime scene tape as they walked back and forth between their police vehicles and the house. Uniformed officers were keeping the media hounds from trying to break down the barricades.

When I went outside, Eddie called the police and told them what we had discovered. Fortunately, Robin had been assigned as head detective. After David was rushed to the hospital, Eddie and I were questioned and let go. "I'll let you guys know what happened the minute we find something," my brother had assured us.

The silence was too hard to bear. I had to break it. "Eddie, I'm so sorry," I said, swallowing the huge lump forming in my throat.

He glanced over at me. "It's not your fault," he said. "Someone nearly killed David, and we didn't get there in time"

"No," I said blinking back the tears, "I'm not talking about that. I don't know what came over me. I just froze back there, and when you yelled at me—." A dark time in my past surged up in my memory, but I pushed it back into the secret, forgotten corners of my mind.

"Shelly." Eddie took one of his hands off the wheel and pulled me close to him. "I didn't mean to yell at you." His voice cracked with emotion as he spoke. "I was more concerned about getting David to the hospital and was frustrated. I should have been there sooner."

Over an hour later, Eddie and I were the only people sitting in the waiting area of Zephyr Memorial Hospital's ER room. I was sitting down in one of the puke green chairs, aimlessly flipping through a two-year copy of Magical Family magazine while Eddie paced back and forth nervously on the worn, steel grey carpet. David's bloodied and bruised body. The dark, red blood on the floor. Those images wouldn't leave my mind, no matter how hard I tried.

I tossed the magazine aside and looked up at my shirtless fiancé. That's when I noticed a small tattoo below his left shoulder blade. It was an image of a billowing green cloak with two daggers crisscrossing the middle of the cloak. Right under the cloak was the number 257. "I didn't know you had a tattoo," I said quietly.

Eddie stopped pacing and flopped down into the seat next to me. "Oh, that? I got it as a requirement when I joined the Agency. Each agent was given a number along with the Agency's symbol."

"Why the tattoo?"

"The ink is physically and magically indestructible. If one of the agents was ever killed, his tattoo would identify him to other agents without blowing his cover." He paused for a few minutes. "You know, David was the one who got me the job with the Agency. Even when I royally screwed up some of my assignments, he was always there for me." He leaned back in his seat and ran his fingers through his curly hair with one hand. Tears began welling up in his eyes, and he wiped them away with the back of his other hand.

I couldn't think of anything comforting to say, so I put my arms around him and leaned against him. We were silent for a few minutes until the ER doctor on duty came out to the waiting room.

"Mr. Van Helsing?" he asked.

I let go of Eddie, and he got up from his seat. "That's me."

"Once again, how exactly are you related to Mr. Endora?"

"Marriage," the vampire lied. It was the only way to know about David's medical prognosis. "How's my uncle?"

"I'm Dr. Gandalf. I'm afraid I have some bad news: Due to the extent of your uncle's injuries, we had to place him in a drug-induced coma."

Eddie's face turned even paler than his already pale skin. "What? Why?"

The doctor hesitated. "Your uncle's injuries are very severe. He has a punctured lung, several deep stab wounds, severe blood loss, three broken ribs, a major concussion—."

"But you're a wizard, you can heal him!" Eddie snapped.

"Eddie," I said calmly as I placed a hand on his arm.

Dr. Gandalf held up his hands. He must have seen this reaction occur every day. "Yes, I am, Mr. Van Helsing, but the drug-induced coma is necessary. Your uncle's body will heal faster this way with little chance of permanent damage."

Eddie sighed. "I'm sorry for my outburst, doctor. Can we see him?"

The doctor nodded and led us down a nearby hall. He opened the door to Room 313. Eddie and I both gasped.

The unconscious wizard was lying in an elevated bed with a bandage around his newly shaved head. The slow and steady beeping of the vital signs monitor echoed throughout the quiet room. He was breathing with the aid of a ventilator, and an IV with fluids and blood was hooked up to him.

"How long is he going to be like this?" Eddie asked.

Dr. Gandalf hesitated. "We don't know. The drug we have put him under will help reduce the swelling in his brain. We'll wake him up now and then, but it is up to your uncle to bring himself out of the coma." He excused himself and left us all alone.

"Shelly, I should take you home," Eddie said, unable to tear his eyes away from David.

I nodded, not wanting to argue with my fiancé. He was very upset. We left the hospital and drove to my house in silence. Right before I got out, I gave Eddie a tight hug. "You going to be okay?"

He managed a nod. "Yeah," he lied.

"Call me if you need to talk."

Chapter Nine:

I Plead For David's Life With the Camelot Society

"Oh, boy!" I said as I read the next morning's headline. "Eddie is not going to like this one bit."

The *Zephyr Herald* shouted a brazen, accusing statement: Local Philanthropist Practices Black Magic. According to the article, an unknown source reported that David was a closet black-magic practitioner. Once David regained consciousness, the Camelot Society was going to revoke his magic privileges.

I swallowed hard. This was bad, very bad. The Camelot Society is an elite group of wizards and enchantresses who more or less monitor other Welkies' magic. They have the power to revoke all of the magical abilities of any Welkie. If the suspected Welkie is practicing illegal, black magic, the magic removal is permanent and sometimes deadly.

According to scientists, there is an area of the cerebral cortex in a Welkie's brain that controls their magical abilities. If a Welkie is found guilty of using black magic, then the Camelot Society will force them to undergo a lobotomy to remove that area of the brain. Unfortunately, not many people survive this procedure and those that do suffer permanent brain damage. If the Camelot Society found David guilty of using black magic, a lobotomy in his current condition could kill him. "I have to do something."

I was nervous at work all day, and this time it wasn't the weird guy having a three-person conversation with himself and his other two personalities. While shelving in the self-help section, I decided to voice my opinion about David at the Zephyr-area Camelot Society.

At five-thirty, I found myself staring up at the twenty-two-story skyscraper. Somewhere on one of those floors was the office of the Camelot Society, deciding the fate of Welkies everywhere in this fair city. I swallowed hard. "Here goes nothing." I pushed open the glass revolving door and walked through the metal detectors and across the pink granite floor to the huge oak desk where a bored-looking Winged One security guard sat with his feet on the desk and the paper in his hands. His ill-fitting black uniform was covered in orange cheese-puff flakes. Mind you, Winged Ones are humanoid creatures with bird-like wings sprouting from their shoulders. Some people compare them to angels, but I think of them like Hawkman and Hawkgirl, minus the dumb masks and the various weapons.

"Excuse me, sir," I said.

"What do ya want, lady?" he asked without looking up from the paper.

"I'm looking for the Camelot Society."

"Twentieth floor. Elevator's on your left."

"Thank you," I said with a nod to the ever-vigilant security guard. Ted Kaczynski could walk past him without any trouble and blow up the entire building.

I pressed the up-button and waited a few moments for the elevator. The doors opened up and I stepped inside. My eyes saw all the buttons, but I resisted the temptation to press every single one. This was too important to fool around right now. I pressed the twentieth button and drew a deep breath. I began to silently rehearse my speech to the Society as the annoying elevator music trilled in the speakers above me.

The doors opened, and I stepped out into a beautiful carpeted office with three doors all guarded by a huge oak desk and a rather imposing, no nonsense elfin secretary. She looked up at me through her bifocals. "Yes?"

"My name is Shelly Anderson. I would like to speak to the members of the Camelot Society."

She began typing on the computer. "Do you have an appointment?"

"No, I didn't know I needed one."

"They are only available by appointment."

"Look," I said firmly. "I need to speak with them about David Endora!"

Her pinched face formed a surprised O. "Let me see if

they are in!" She pressed a button on her phone. "Mr. Elymas?"

"Yes, Edna?"

"There is a Ms. Shelly Anderson here to speak with the Camelot Society about David Endora."

Two female and another male voices conferred with the first speaker. "Show her in."

Edna pointed to the first door. "Thank you," I said. I took a deep breath and knocked on the heavy oak door.

"Come in!" commanded a deep voice.

I pushed the door open and stepped inside. It looked more like a courtroom than a conference room. Three Welkies sat behind four, austere judge benches surrounding one small table and a chair. A witness stand stood off to the left of the table and chair. The lighting was poor, and it seemed like an interrogation room.

The Welkie in the middle was Harrison Elymas, the supreme justice of the Zephyr City Court. He stared at me with piercing gray eyes. Robin had told me he was a no-nonsense judge who never bent the rules on anything. "Ms. Anderson, I understand that you have some information about David

Endora."

I nodded, feeling like I was in the principal's office. "Yes, sir."

"Well, tell us."

I glanced nervously at the old woman on the right. She was Phyllis Merlinson, Zephyr's ambassador to the nearby city-states. It was rumored she'd stopped a civil war by staring down the opposing leaders without uttering a single word. "All right." I took a deep breath and exhaled slowly. "I read in the paper the Camelot Society was going to revoke his magical abilities."

"Yes, that's true," said the third member of the Camelot Society, none other than Leon Laveau.

"Well," I said, "I know David would never practice black magic. He abhors it."

Laveau steepled his hands together and rested his chin on them. "We never truly know someone, do we?"

"But there must be some kind of mistake!" I protested. "David hates black magic. He has told me and my fiancé this on several occasions."

Elymas raised a perfect eyebrow at me. "What is your relationship with Mr. Endora, Ms. Anderson?"

"He's my fiancé's mentor."

"And your fiancé would be?"

"Eddie Van Helsing."

Laveau looked at Elymas and Merlinson. "Endora's poster-boy vampire for Carpe Noctum," he informed them. "I regret giving Endora money for his philanthropic effort, even after what he did to the mayor and his wife with that thing."

"David didn't kill the mayor!" I snapped.

"Ms. Anderson, one more outburst, and I will have to ask you to leave," Elamas said sternly, but his eyes softened. He must have seen the exasperation on my face. "Ms. Anderson, I understand you want to help Mr. Endora, but I'm afraid there's nothing you can do."

"What do you mean?" I asked.

"We have photographs proving his involvement in the practice of black magic," Elymas replied.

"Can I see them?"

They all shook their heads. "The contributor who wishes

to remain anonymous requested the pictures remain private,"
Laveau said.

I frowned. Someone must have definitely set my friend up, but for what purpose? "If I can prove that David isn't practicing black magic, will you let him keep his powers?"

They all gave me a patronizing smile. "Okay, my dear," Merlinson said as if I were a small child. "You play detective, but as you may know, pictures tell a thousand words."

Did she think I was some kind of Encyclopedia Brown wanna-be? My friend's life was on the line, and she thought I was playing a game. My mouth started moving before my brain could tell it to shut up. "When do you want my proof?"

The Welkies looked at each other and began to confer in whispered tones, completely ignoring my presence. Finally, they all looked at me. "You may present your 'proof' next Thursday night at seven-thirty," Elymas told me.

Once again, my mouth opened before conferring with my brain. "I'll be there with proof of David's innocence." After they waved me from the room as if I was some kind of peasant, the realization hit me. What did I just agree to? I asked myself. And what am I going to do about it? Clearly, I didn't think this through

as carefully as I had thought.

Eddie didn't answer his phone when I left him a message,

detailing my experience with the Camelot Society. At

eleven-thirty that night I was just about to fall asleep when my

cell phone jarred me awake. After a few moments of blindly

fumbling around my nightstand, I answered it. "Hello?" I asked.

"Shelly," Eddie said wasting no time getting his point, "be

ready to go by two."

"In the morning?"

"Yes."

"Why?"

"Because we are going to prove David's innocence. Dress

completely in black."

I rubbed my eyes with my free hand. "Why?"

"Because we might be doing something illegal."

"Wow!" I said impressed. "Usually, I'm the one suggesting

illegal activities."

I detected a faint smile in the vampire's voice. "Just be

ready at two, okay?"

"I'll be ready!" I hung up the phone and reset my alarm for one-thirty. But I couldn't sleep at all. My mind kept guessing about Eddie's plans. At one o'clock, I crawled out of bed and threw on a black long sleeved tee and black jeans. I rummaged around my room for my black sneakers and black socks. I pulled my hair back into a ponytail and brushed my teeth. I checked my watch. One-thirty. I called Eddie. "If you want me to come along, you better bring some coffee."

"Got it!"

Right on time, Eddie arrived at my house. I grabbed my keys and phone and ran out the door. Opening up the passenger door of Eddie's carrot car, I climbed in as Eddie handed me a black baseball cap and a cup of iced caramel coffee. I took a gulp. Two creams, two sugars. Just the way I like it.

"Morning," Eddie said.

"Morning," I said with a yawn. Setting my coffee in a cup holder, I put on the baseball cap and pulled my ponytail through the hole in the back. I glanced at the vampire's attire. A black knit cap was pulled over his ears. He was wearing a black turtleneck, black jeans, and his black motorcycle boots. His black motorcycle gloves gripped the steering wheel as he turned it out of my driveway. "Okay, what are we doing?" I asked him. "Special Ops?"

"You said in your message the Camelot Society had photos proving David's involvement with black magic, right?" I nodded. "Well, we're going to do some investigating at David's house."

"Isn't that illegal?"

"And falsely accusing David of practicing black magic is legal?" Eddie snapped at me without thinking.

"Sorry," I said softly.

He glanced at me and squeezed my knee. "It's not your fault, babe. I've just been really worried about David."

"Any change?"

"No," Eddie said, "I sat with him for about three hours today. Still no change."

"He's going to recover, right?"

"They don't know. But I can't just sit around and do

nothing. If David does wake up and the Camelot Society finds him guilty, he could die from the Society's lobotomy! I have to prove his innocence!" Eddie let go of my knee and hit the top of the steering wheel with the heel of his hand in frustration.

"Don't worry, Eddie. We will."

Eddie pulled the car around the back of David's house. "Let's go!" He grabbed two flashlights and a small camera from the back seat. He tossed one of the flashlights to me.

I glanced longingly at my coffee before getting out of the car. I followed my vampire to the back door which was sealed off in crime scene tape. That didn't stop Eddie who ducked under it and let himself in. I followed him and turned on my light. The hallway was still covered in dried blood, and my mind could still see the injured wizard on the floor. I shut my eyes to block out the image.

"Shelly!" Eddie said breathlessly from David's study. Something had shocked him. "Take a look at this!"

I walked into the nearby study where David had been teaching sword fighting and gasped at what I saw. On the hardwood floor and inside a bloody circle, someone had painted the black outline of a hand with a bolt of lightning streaking across of the palm. Something in the back of my mind nagged at me. I had seen that image somewhere before, but on a smaller scale. "Eddie," I asked, not taking my eyes away from the image, "is that—."

He nodded as if he were in a trance. "A symbol of black magic." He fell to his knees and sniffed the blood. "No, it can't be David's! It just can't be!"

I swallowed hard. Using blood in any type of spell is a big no-no, and if you use your own blood, then you are a master of black magic. "Are you sure, Eddie?" According to my fiancé, each person has a distinct smell to their blood only vampires can detect. But maybe he was wrong.

"It's David's blood. I can smell the herbal tea he drinks."

Something glinted off my flashlight beam near the desk. It was the shield bracelet that the wizard was going to give me at my next lesson. The metal bracelet was almost identical to the ones Wonder Woman wore, except for one small detail. On the bracelet's underside was a small button. When you pressed it, an indestructible, three-foot metal shield popped out. The round shield's front was emblazoned with a blue lion surrounded by three fleurs-de-les. When I first saw the shield, I knew I had seen that symbol once before, but for the life of me, I still hadn't figured out where. I walked to the desk and picked the bracelet off the floor. David was supposed to give it to me during one of my lessons, but the bracelet had a broken clasp. I looked it over before putting it on my left wrist. I pressed the button, and the shield popped up. "David must have fixed it."

Eddie looked over at me. "Where did you get that?"

"On the floor."

"He must have dropped it."

"Not intentionally! This is a really expensive shield bracelet. It once belonged to an ancient line of royal warriors." David had told me the name of the warrior race, but I couldn't remember it at the moment. I pressed the bracelet's button and lowered the shield. "David wouldn't just drop something like this."

"His attacker must have startled him while he was fixing your shield."

I glanced down at a piece of paper on the desk. At first, it looked like a recipe, but when I read it more carefully, I realized it was instructions for a potion. "Eddie, look at this!"

He came over and read the list aloud. "Two newt eyes, three dragon scales, one cup of ground hogweed, and a tablespoon of harpy blood. Mix all ingredients in a flame-resistant container. Repeat the following phrase three times: Fiend of the underworld, arise and do my bidding!" He dropped the paper in shock. "Shelly, do you realize what this is?"

I shook my head. "No, what is it?"

"A death ray summoning spell!"

"What's a death ray?"

Eddie shrugged. "Never seen one before, but if I recall my black magic history, summoning a death ray is one of the highest forms of black magic!" He looked around the study. "Let's get out of here before someone sees us!"

We hurried back to the car. "This doesn't make any sense," I said to Eddie as we drove back to my house.

Eddie nodded in reply. "Something's off about the whole thing."

"Okay, you said that summoning this creature is one of the

highest forms of black magic. So, why go from performing good magic to black magic in no time?”

“Are you saying that David is guilty of black magic? He’s not a killer!”

“Of course not! I’m just confused on how someone could go from wizard to sorcerer in less than a week.”

“How do you know that exact timeline?”

“I had a lesson at his house last week, and there was no evidence of black magic.”

Eddie considered that fact for a moment. “What’s also odd about this whole thing is how everything is clear cut.”

“You mean like the huge symbol and black magic spell out in plain sight?”

“Yeah!”

“Hypothetically speaking, if David were practicing black magic, wouldn’t he have done it at some secluded place and not in his own house out in the open for all to see?”

“And the handwriting is David’s, but it isn’t.”

It had sure looked like David’s handwriting to me. “What do you mean?”

"When I was training to be a spy with the Agency, I took a couple courses in handwriting analysis. Each person has a distinct penmanship style which tells a lot about him or her. David's a perfectionist. He writes very, very carefully."

I thought about it for a minute. Three of the words on the piece of paper had been crossed out and then corrected. "If David had really written the spell, there would have been no mistakes!"

Eddie nodded as he pulled the car to a stop in front of my house. "It's a set-up! It has to be!"

"But who would do this and why?"

Chapter Ten:

Someone Takes Out Barbie Spellman

The next morning, Professor Faraday left me a voicemail about the substance on my shoe. Apparently, the junk came from a reptilian-like water creature's nasal passages. The creature, known as a Gojira, has boogers which are toxic for five hours after leaving the nasal pouch, located beneath the lower jaw.

At work, I decided to do a little research on this creature. Unfortunately, we had one book on Gojiras which had been checked out for ten years. Translation: it was never coming back to the library, not in my lifetime anyway. I even tried looking on the internet, but there was very little information on the creature. According to one fairly reliable article, Gojiras are very camera shy and almost always eat the photographers who try to take pictures of them. The few pictures of the survivors were too out of focus to get a decent description of the sea monster. Marine biologists did discover a head of a Gojira and were able to analyze what the nasal cavities did, but that was about it for scientific discovery.

I was on my lunch break sending Eddie an email about the toxic mucus when I overheard the head of special collections, Carla, talking to General Mothman. "Well, I hope your friend got everything that he needed from The Black Magic Grimoire, General Mothman."

"Of course, Carla, and thank you for letting me borrow it."

Once Mothman left, I looked up the call number of the book on one of the office computers. After jotting the number down on a piece of scrap paper, I headed down into the library's basement where we keep the non-circulating books. The non-circulation collection, or as we lovingly call it "the cage," is a maze of organized chaos of old books and bound periodicals stashed away on dusty metal bookcases. After wandering the stacks for a few moments, I decided to locate Carla. She was sitting at large desk cluttered with more old books, maps, a pencil holder made from an old soup can, a stapler, and one lone desktop computer. "Carla, I was wondering if I could take a look at The Black Magic Grimoire," I told her. "Someone wants some information for research."

The dwarf raised a gray eyebrow. "My, that is a popular book today."

I shrugged. "How about that?"

"Come with me," I followed the dwarf to the bookcase that I must have passed three times. She pointed down to the last shelf at an old, blue bound book that was about six inches thick. "That's the one," Carla said. She was about to say something when someone paged her over the intercom, and she hurried away.

I squatted down and lifted the book off the shelf. I sat on a nearby stool and looked at the book. There were only two dog-eared pages in the entire book, and I opened up to the first book marker and inhaled deeply.

It was the exact same spell we saw on David's desk. But it was the picture next to the spell that made me reel back in astonishment. It was the same, one-eyed, one-horn, flying, purple, people vaporizer who made a surprise, but deadly visit to the ballgame. So that was a death ray.

Using my finger as a bookmark, I turned to the next dog-eared page. I gave a low whistle as I read the next spell's ingredients: one cup of human blood, two tablespoons of coral snake venom, one-fourth cup of fly agaric mushrooms, and two cups of ground cherry and peach pits. The incantation said something about raising the likeness of another being and making it your minion. A tall, anorexic, Roswell alien was pictured next to the spell.

I had heard about dopplegangers. They, like zombies, are created with black magic but are more easily controlled by their maker. Also, they have the nasty habit of ripping open the chest of their victims with their unbreakable, retractable razor-sharp claws. Dopplegangers also have the ability to morph into anyone or anything. The only distinguishing feature is their completely black eyes. And I'm not talking about the iris. Their entire eyeballs are coal black.

This was bad, bad like computer blue screen of death

bad. I took the spellbook over to the nearby photocopier and make two copies of both spells for me and Eddie, before reshelving the book.

I was driving down my street when I first saw the flashing blue lights. "What the?" I pulled the car over to the side of the road and walked towards the police barrier that was right in front of my driveway. I spotted my brother squatting down beside something lying on the gravel. Parked on the side of the street was a covered, winged-horse drawn carriage, the mobile Crime Scene Unit.

"Shelly!" Someone hissed.

I turned to see Quentin poking his head from behind his stable. He beckoned me over with one of his talons. "What's going on?" I asked the griffin when I arrived.

"Someone killed Ruby!"

Ruby? Who was Ruby, the tabloid reporter's alter ego? "Do you know who did it?"

"Some guy dressed in a delivery uniform."

I raised an eyebrow. "Why would a delivery man kill

someone? Unless, they never picked up their package. Come on," I told the griffin. "Let's go tell the police."

He grabbed the strap of my purse with his beak and pulled me back. "You can't!"

"Why not!"

"Because everyone will think I killed her when she refused to turn me back into a superstar."

I gave an eyeroll. "Right, I forgot. Okay, what did this guy look like?"

"I didn't get a good look at his face, except for his eyes. They were completely black."

I sucked in a breath of air. The killer was a doppelganger. "Look, go hide in the stable, and I'll find out what happened." I shooed the griffin off and walked up to the police barricade.

An overweight, uniformed satyr held up his hand to stop me from going any further. What did he think I was going to do? Pull a Steve McQueen and jump the barricade? "What's going on?" I asked nonchalantly.

"This is none of your concern, missy," the officer said. "This is police business."

"That's in front of my house."

"I'm sorry, but I can't let you through."

Robin looked up from the driveway. "Hermes, it's okay." He got to his feet and walked over to me. "She's my sister."

"What's going on, Robin?" I asked my brother.

He took out a notepad and a pen as he took on a very professional manner. "I understand you and Eddie had a confrontation with Barbie Spellman at the festival the other day."

I raised an eyebrow. "Yeah, we didn't like her taking pictures of us without our permission and writing that scathing article. Why do you want to know?"

"Someone killed her by ripping her chest open."

I glanced over at the body. "And you think I killed her? By ripping her chest open?"

My brother sighed, his cop-mode giving way to older-brother-mode. "Of course not, Shelly, it's just protocol, you know that."

"I didn't kill her, and neither did Eddie."

Robin nodded. "So, just to make things clear, where have you been today?"

"At work, and my coworkers can vouch for me."

"What about Eddie?"

"He sleeps during the day until three or four before leaving for work from six to three."

He nodded as he put away his notebook. "I'll talk to him before he heads off to work." He turned to go, but stopped as if he remembered something. "There was some stuff on her camera."

"Like what? The picture in the paper?"

"Not just that one. There were more."

"More?"

"Yeah." He called over to one of the crime scene techs who was bagging evidence and asked them to bring over two bags with Barbie Spellman's camera and a small cell phone. After taking the camera out of the bag, he turned it on and scrolled through the pictures on the LCD screen.

"What the?" I asked as I looked in shock at the various pictures. The images consisted of me going to and from work, running errands, and the occasional one of me and Eddie on a date.

"Did you know about any of these?" Robin asked.

I shook my head as a shiver ran up my spine. "I only knew about the pictures she took at the tennis court."

"So, you have no idea about any of these pictures?"

"No!" My hands started shaking. This went way beyond an undignified front page picture. Barbie Spellman had been stalking me, but to what purpose? "What was she doing?"

"I don't know, but—." He paused and drew in a long breath before slowly exhaling. "She was also carrying this." He pulled out the phone and turned on the email application. "We plugged the memory chip into the mobile computer, and found out she had been sending the pictures to this email address before she showed up in Zephyr."

I shook my head. "Who was she sending them to?"

"Don't know. One of the tech guys said the IP address is untraceable. But whoever she was in contact with had a substantial amount of money. Someone was dropping five grand into her bank account for every picture."

"Can you trace it?"

He shook his head. "We're trying, but it looks like the

person behind all this was using a false identity."

"Wow!" I said, shaking my head in disbelief.

"Talk to Eddie about it. He might have an idea. Whoever was doing this probably worked at the Agency with him."

I managed a nod. "Can I go?"

"Sure, I'll call you or Eddie if I learn anything else."

I walked back to Quentin who was cowardly hiding in his shed. "So, who killed her, Shelly?" he asked me.

"They don't know, Quentin," I told him. I decided not to impart the new-found knowledge that someone had employed Barbie to stalk me. I saddled up and climbed on Quentin's back. "Take me to my dad's restaurant."

I had never seen Anderson's Place so crowded since the week Dad first opened. Even all the spots in the employee parking lot behind the diner were taken. I jumped off Quentin. "Go home," I told him.

"Why?"

"So, that you can see if the killer comes back."

He gave me a skeptical look. "Would that actually

happen?"

"Oh, yeah," I lied. "They always come back to the scene of the crime. Something in their criminal pathology, I understand. Killers like to relive the crime scene over and over again."

The griffin's eyes lit up with excitement. He saluted me with his right claw. "Yes, ma'am!" He began to furiously beat his wings. "Never fear! Quentin the Great will keep an eye out for the killer." With that overconfident statement, he gave a running start before he took off into the night sky.

I went in through the front door, a big mistake on my part. I maneuvered my way past the large group of people and television reporters who were surrounding a table in the center of the restaurant. And sitting at that table with a news camera in front of him was Laveau.

"Councilman Laveau, is it true your opponent does not have a spotless military record as he has claimed?"

The wizard gave his award-winning smile before answering the reporter. "That is true, Mark. According to my sources, he was court-martialed for mishandling a raid on Diablo Island. General Mothman has betrayed our fair city once, and the good people of Zephyr must not let him do it again."

The reporter nodded faithfully. No doubt that last sentence was going to be played over and over again all over the news. "General Mothman has told us you knew of David Endora's black magic practices and have been covering up all along."

Fury flashed in Laveau's eyes, but I couldn't tell if it was real or practiced anger. "Nobody knew Mr. Endora was a sorcerer. I was absolutely shocked when I found out. Had I known, I never would have invested in his corporation."

A waiter came over to the table balancing a tray filled with food. "Here's your garden fresh salad, Mr. Laveau," the pimply-face teenager said as he began to set the tray on down a tray table.

Eddie came rushing out of the kitchen and over to the table. He grabbed the tray from the waiter. "Greg, you forgot to put Mr. Laveau's salad dressing on the side," he said. The vampire shot the wizard a fake smile. "I'll take care of this, sir."

I knew my fiancé was up to no good, and so I followed him back into the kitchen. I touched his arm as he set the tray on a counter. "Eddie, please tell me you're not going to put something nasty in his food."

Eddie leaned against the counter. "I should, Shelly. Laveau is making David out to be an evil sorcerer. He knows David is innocent because he's somehow behind all of this. Laveau is lying to the press."

"He's a politician, Eddie. What do you expect? Look, I know that you don't like Laveau. But if you do anything to his food, Dad might find out, and he won't be a happy camper."

Eddie sighed. "I know." He stared down at the tray, debating whether or not to leave an unexpected present in the salad.

"You're going to resist tampering with the salad, right?"

He managed a smile. "Of course, I am." He gathered up the tray and started to head out to the dining room.

I sighed with relief. I decided to tell him the unsettling news I had just received. "Uh, Eddie."

He paused as he turned to face me. "Yeah, Shell?"

"I found out some rather disturbing things today."

"Like what?"

I hesitated. "Just finish up what you're doing, and I'll tell you afterwards."

Eddie noticed my suddenly shaking hands I was trying to hide by crossing my arms. He flagged down a fellow employee and handed the salad to him. "Chuck, take this out to Mr. Laveau at table six."

"Sure, Eddie," Chuck said as he took the tray and walked out the swinging doors.

The vampire turned to me. "What's going on?"

The full shock of what I had learned earlier hit me like a brick, and I staggered back. "I-I need to sit down."

Eddie caught my elbow and led me outside to his car. Once we were inside, he looked at me with concern. "What happened, Shell?"

I glanced around the parking lot to make sure nobody was watching us. All clear. I took a deep breath to ease my rapid heartbeat before I told him everything that had transpired.

Eddie was holding me close to him. "Robin's sure someone was paying Barbie Spellman to take pictures of you?"

I managed a nod. "Yeah, the person is really good. He's untraceable." I leaned my head against his shoulder. "I don't know who would want to do this to me."

"Whoever it was might have been trying to get to me."

"You think that it might be one of your enemies from the Agency? Robin suggested the same thing."

He shrugged. "Maybe. I still have contacts at the Agency. I'll give them a call tomorrow." He looked at me with his gentle green eyes. "I won't let anyone hurt you. I promise." He cupped my chin in his hands and gave me a loving kiss.

"I know you won't." I relaxed a bit when I remembered something. "Oh, my gosh!"

"What?"

"I just figured something out. Do you remember the image we saw at David's?"

"Yeah, how could I forget?"

"I saw the exact same symbol when I was at Diablo Island."

"Yeah, but the symbol you saw was probably pretty old. Rumors about black magic have always been associated with Diablo Island."

I shook my head. "I don't think so."

Eddie shot me a quizzical look. "What are you thinking?"

"It's just that Diablo Island has been coming up a lot in conversations lately. And these conversations are all connected to David and the mayoral candidates in one way or another. Maybe the only way to figure out this whole mess is to check the island out."

Eddie nodded. "I know a guy who rents speedboats down by the docks. I'll give him a call to see if we can borrow one tomorrow night after I get out of work."

I looked at him in horror. "At two in the morning?"

Eddie gave me a little smirk. "It'll prepare you for living with a vampire."

I rolled my eyes. "How, on these rare occasions, is prying my butt out of bed five hours earlier than normal going to prepare me for sleeping during the day and being awake during the night?"

"Do you want to make this a routine?"

"No!" I gave a defeated sigh. "Well, if I'm going to be getting up at an ungodly hour, coffee better be involved."

He smiled. "As you wish."

Eddie took me home on his lunch break. He even had me stay in the car while he checked out my house for any signs of possible intruders. Even after my fiancé declared the place safe and secure, I still felt afraid. I mean, someone had paid Barbie Spellman to spy on me. I had seen a lot of scary things since I've lived here in Zephyr, but learning about an unknown stalker really freaked me out. It took me a long time to fall asleep.

Chapter Eleven:
From Hospital Visit to Blockbuster Movie

My cell phone woke up me out of a fitful sleep at five the next morning. "Hello?" I asked sleepily.

"Michelle Topaz Anderson!" There is one person in the world who uses my full name in that authoritative voice.

"Dad, what's going on?" I asked.

"Your brother just told me about Barbie Spellman stalking you. Why didn't you tell me?"

"I told Eddie."

"You should have told me first."

I was glad that Dad couldn't see my eye-roll. I love my dad, but he has a tendency to be a little overprotective. Probably because I am his little girl. "Dad, I'm okay!"

"Do you want to stay with your stepmother and me until this whole thing gets sorted out?"

"Dad, I'm okay. Eddie took me home last night and made sure that I was safe."

I didn't catch what my stepmom said in the background, but Dad did and apparently didn't like it. "Not now, Amelia," he said firmly.

"What was that all about?" I asked him.

"Um, we're having a little argument about what color we should paint the living room."

That was a lie. They had painted the living room three weeks ago. I decided not to pursue the subject anymore. "Look, Dad, don't worry. It's probably one of the creepy people at work, or someone Eddie knew. He's going to call some of his contacts at the Agency."

Dad sighed. "Okay, I just wanted to make sure you're all right."

"Dad, I have to go."

"Stay safe, sweetheart."

"You worry too much."

"I have to. I'm your father."

"I'll be careful. Talk to you later, Dad."

"Bye, Shelly."

"Bye, Dad." I hung up the phone and lay back in bed. I closed my eyes and tried to fall back asleep. Glancing at my alarm clock which was glaring the bright digits of 5:10, I realized that I had two options. I could go back to bed and sleep for another hour and twenty minutes or I could get up and be ready for work an hour earlier than normal. My mind wanted the first option, but my body won in favor of the second option. I rolled out of bed and got ready for the day.

After work, I decided to visit David in the hospital. This was going to be the first time I had seen the wizard on my own. I know I should have seen him earlier, but I just didn't know what to say. I had grabbed a book by one of his favorite poets from the library. The least I could do was read to him. The floor of the intensive care unit was uneasily quiet. I saw Dr. Gandalf, David's attending physician, talking to the nurse sitting at the lobby check-in desk.

"How's David Endora?" I asked them as I signed my name on the visitor sign-in sheet that was attached to a clipboard.

"Still the same," Gandalf said.

"Is it all right to see him?"

The doctor nodded. He turned to the elfin nurse and started to discuss the conditions of another patient.

I walked into the hospital room and froze at what I saw. With his back to me, I saw Dr. Gandalf preparing to slice the wire to David's respirator with a pair of wirecutters. Either the good doctor had just decided to do his medical practice Kevorkian-style or he had an evil twin. "What are you doing?" I asked him.

Dr. Gandalf dropped the wire and turned to face me. The complete emptiness of his black eyes betrayed his disguise. Dr. Gandalf snarled at me. Last time I checked, Welkies had normal teeth, not three rows of extreme sharp teeth. Crap! It was the doppelganger.

I pressed the button on my bracelet, and the shield appeared just in time as the creature vaulted over the bed at me like some kind of mutant gymnast. He slammed feet first onto my shield, knocking me on my backside. That was going to hurt later.

I scrambled to my feet and ran after him as he bolted out the door. Had I not been practicing my sword fighting, I would have been wheezing and out of breath by the time I had followed the creature into the stairwell. I was surprised at how empty the hall was. No doctors, no nurses. Then again, the doppelganger was noiseless on his feet.

The doppelganger stopped on the next level only for a moment. I watched in fascinated horror as it sliced itself from the top of it head, down alongside its face, then made a "Y" incision and made a long slice down each leg. It began slithering back and forth and emerged a tall, thin, alien-like creature. It was tossing the Dr. Gandalf skin aside when it saw me and began running away, taking the stairs three at a time.

Two options lay before me: I could alert hospital security or chase the creature. I took the stupid option. I put away the poetry book, pulled my book out of my purse, hoisted the purse up onto my shoulder, and said, "Knowledge is power." Within moments, the book had changed into my sword, and I began running after the doppelganger.

In my head, I imagined catching the creature and fighting him off with my sword and shield. But reality has a nasty habit of stomping on your imagination and grinding it into the floor with the heel of disappointment. When I reached the next floor, I didn't realize I was stepping on the extremely dry skin until my feet went out from under me. My purse slid off my shoulder, and everything, but the kitchen sink, spilled onto the stairs. I dropped Knowledge so I wouldn't impale myself. My fanny hit the stairs hard, and I frantically grabbed the railing as I slid down a couple more steps.

The door at the bottom of the stairs slammed shut. I attempted to resume the chase by standing. Pain started to radiate through my elbow, my left arm, and butt. I slowly deactivated the shield and collected the contents of my purse. I winced in pain as I picked up my sword and looked it over. No dents. Impressive. "Without Knowledge, there is no Power," I said, and the sword turned back into a book. I hobbled down to the next level.

I found a nurses' station and told them what had happened. "We'll have security check the building, Ms. Anderson." She eyed me. "Are you all right?"

"Well, I might have bruised my tailbone, my left arm, and elbow."

"Let's get you checked out to make sure that nothing's broken." They took a couple of x-rays which show only bruises, and sent me off with a bottle of silver unicorn pills. Silver unicorn horns have a magical healing power. The ground powder comes in pill form as well as a topical substance and will heal anything from massive head wounds to broken bones. The downside is that it makes you really drowsy and takes about five hours for the full healing process to take effect. It's like having your medicine injected with Wolverine's healing ability.

I hobbled out to my car, went to the drive-thru at Mac's, and ordered a BBQ chicken wrap and a soda before heading home. By the time I got to my front door, my hands were shaking terribly. I glanced around for Quentin, but the griffin was nowhere in sight. He was probably out hunting. After fumbling with the lock and dropping my keys about five times, I finally got inside,

took the recommended dose of the unicorn pills, ate my meal,

and crawled into bed.

Chapter Twelve:
Eddie and I Nearly Die in a Speedboat

My cell phone rang waking me from a deep sleep. After knocking it off my nightstand, I retrieved it and flipped it open. "Hello?"

"Shelly, did you forget about our excursion tonight?" Eddie asked.

I glanced at my alarm clock. It read three-ten. "Oh, crap! I forgot to set my alarm. I'm so sorry, Eddie. Where are you?"

"Don't worry about it, Shell. I'm sitting in your driveway."

I ran my fingers through my hair. "Okay, just let yourself in." After hanging up, I rolled out of bed and went to the bathroom. Looking in the mirror, I realized no comb would tame my bedraggled hair, short of washing it with shampoo and conditioner. Thank God for hats. I heard Eddie come through the front door, and I went out to greet him.

The vampire had changed out of his work clothes and was now wearing a pair of faded blue jeans with his black motorcycle boots. Under the jean jacket I got for him one Christmas, he was wearing a black AC-DC T-shirt. Even though he was looking fine as always, what he was holding in his hands caught my eye. A drink tray holding two cups and a flat box. He set everything down on my kitchen table.

"Ooh, you brought coffee and doughnuts!" I took the cup marked with my name and took a sip. Just the way I like my coffee: caramel swirl with two creams and two sugars. "So," I said as I opened the box of doughnuts, "how long were you waiting for me?" There were supposed to be six doughnuts, but three were mysteriously missing.

"About an hour. I called you about three times."

"I didn't hear you."

Eddie smiled. "I did have a moment of stupidity and thought about going into your house to make sure you were okay. But then my brain reminded me if you woke up and I was standing in your bedroom, you would be really creeped out."

I nodded as I took a bite out of a Bavarian doughnut. "Good call there. But I would have only been creeped out for a moment. Then I would've realized it was you, and I would've definitely decked you."

Eddie nodded. "Yep, that exact same scenario played in my mind."

"So, instead of breaking and entering, you decided to eat three doughnuts."

"You should consider me a hero. I ate the glazed ones and left you the good ones."

I stared into the box. There were a few sprinkles, but no matching doughnut. I didn't have to read Eddie's mind to figure out what happened. "You're a bad doughnut liar," I said with a smile. "You ate the only sprinkled doughnut!"

"Yeah, but I got you two Boston crèmes and that Barvarian crème, your favorites."

I rolled my eyes at his logic. "Gee, thanks for saving me from the dangers of a sprinkled doughnut."

He shrugged and kissed me. "That's why I look out for you. I'll get you another sprinkled doughnut."

"Good, but I better come with you in case you eat it."

He started laughing which made me smile. "We better get going. Shamus is waiting for us."

"Okay, let me grab a hat. My hair is a mess." I walked into my bedroom. "Don't you dare eat my doughnuts, Edgar Van Helsing!" I rummaged around until I found a navy blue Zephyr Police baseball hat that Robin gave me. A thought occurred to me. Probably should tell Eddie about the incident at the hospital, I realized. I contemplated how to bring up the subject. "Hey, Eddie!" I called.

"I'm not eating your doughnuts!"

"It's not that. Did you know that dopplegangers use their claws to cut themselves out of their skin?"

Eddie didn't answer for a while. I wondered if he sometimes felt like Ricky Ricardo. Finally, he spoke. "Hunh, I'm guessing you came across this knowledge first-hand."

Thinking it might be cold on the open water, I threw on a light jacket and came out to the kitchen. "Funny story."

Eddie blew out a sigh, waiting for the inevitable. "What did you do?"

I gave him a quick recap of the hospital incident. He listened quietly, holding his tongue until I finished. Finally, he spoke. "You chased after a doppelganger?" he asked incredulously.

"I was armed. I had my sword and shield out."

"You chased after a doppelganger?"

"I can take care of myself."

Eddie ran his fingers through his black, curly hair and sighed. "I know you can, Shell. I'm just impressed you went after a doppelganger. And on your own, for that matter."

"Yeah," I said shaking my head in disbelief at my actions. "Now that I think about it, I guess my brain was taking a short vacation at the time."

He smiled at me. "Either way, I'm still impressed, but the next time you decide to go after a doppelganger, at least give me a heads up first."

By the time we arrived at the docks, we were already an hour and an half late for our appointment. Eddie parked the car under a street light which blinked three times before it went completely out. Looking up the street, I spotted the faded chalk outline of a body on the sidewalk. I looked at Eddie. "Great! I now feel totally safe!"

"You're with me. It doesn't get any safer than this." We walked to the end of Wiltmore Street to a run-down shack that hadn't seen a fresh coat of paint since Elvis performed his first concert. If you filled in the missing letters, the faded blue neon sign read: Shamus' Boats.

Eddie rapped on the front steel door as I peered through one of the barred windows. The door opened.

"Eddie Van Helsing!" Shamus Grizzle greeted us. The tall, burly werebear was wearing a charcoal grey fisherman's sweater, a pair of denim overalls, and a matching knit cap. He looked over his bifocals at us with his brown eyes. "It's good to see you, and this must be your fiancée." He shook my hand with one of his bear paws.

I introduced myself. "So, Eddie tells me he used to work for you."

He took the cigar from his mouth and tapped its end. Ashes floated down to the wooden floor. "Eddie can fix any kind of engine. If one of my motors was out of whack, he would have it up and running in no time." He looked over at Eddie. "Do you want some part-time work, Eddie?"

"Thanks, but no thanks!" the vampire said with a smile.

"Too bad. Could really use the extra hand."

I looked around the boat shop and saw just how bad business was for the werebear. Business hadn't been booming in the last few weeks, and Shamus was behind in his payments.

The shelves hadn't been restocked in a while, and there was even a thin layer of dust on the cash register. When Shamus limped behind the counter, I noticed he was wearing only one boot on his right leg. A wooden peg peeked from the cuff of his left pant leg. He was still getting use to the wooden prosthetic. The time he spent in the hospital three months ago after an unknown sea creature attacked him didn't help his business.

I realized I was reading Shamus' mind without his knowledge and quickly backed out. "So," I said to Eddie, "why don't we go on that boat ride you promised me?"

Shamus smiled. "Ah, young love." He grabbed a set of keys off a key rack and handed them to Eddie. "Don't forget to log in." Dust flew off the cover of a three-ring binder as he opened it to the correct page and then pushed it over to my fiancé.

Eddie took the pen the werebear offered him and signed his name. "Which boat are we getting?"

"The Hummingbird LX. Fastest one out there. I just got her in last week. She's a thirty-footer." He glanced over to the wall with its life jackets. "Need any of those?"
Eddie shook his head. "No, we're fine."

"Yes," I said firmly before the vampire could object any further.

Eddie gave a little shrug. "She's the boss. We'll take two."

After we filled out the rental agreement, Shamus led us to the docks next to his business. Sitting in the water was a long, sleek black speedboat with neon green racing stripes across the top of the bow and along the sides. "There she is!"

"Wow!" Eddie said as he looked up and down the boat. "What's her horsepower?"

"Eight-fifty."

"Nice!" Eddie squatted down to get a closer look at the

twin engines on the back of the boat. After a quick inspection, he stood and looked at me. "These engines are the highest quality out there." Throwing on his life jacket, he practically leaped into the boat and slid into the driver's seat which was on the starboard side. He looked over the dashboard as he buckled himself in. "Oh, this is sweet!" he said excitedly. Eddie was on a roll. He was talking the same way he talks about cars. "Shell, take a look at this thing. It has the works, and even a built-in GPS. Come on in, babe!"

"Okay," I said, taking his word for it. I strapped on my life preserver, buckled all the buttons as tightly as possible and froze. An unexplainable wave of fear and dizziness swept over me. Somewhere in the recesses of my mind, a childhood nightmare resurfaced. A young child getting pushed out of a boat. Dark liquid closes in around her. Two strong hands pull her out of a dark watery demise.

"Shell, are you coming aboard?" Eddie asked me as he united the boat from the dock.

I blinked back into reality. I realized I was gripping one of the dock's wooden pilings to steady myself. The dizziness quickly passed, and I glanced up into the night sky. Even with the moon, the ocean still looked ominous. "Maybe we should get there another way. I can still call Quentin."

"Come on. It'll be fun."

I swallowed my fear and with Eddie's help, stepped into the rocking boat. I sank quickly into the seat and buckled myself in.

Eddie turned the key in the ignition and put the throttle in reverse. The Hummingbird LX slowly began to back out of the harbor. I began to relax. Maybe, this isn't going to be as bad as I thought, I told myself. Once we had cleared the pier, my calming thoughts soon disappeared as the vampire pulled the boat into full throttle. I sucked in my breath as the boat accelerated at the rate of a missile, barely touching the surface of the water. Eddie made three extremely sharp turns. I thought the boat would capsize at any moment.

I gripped the inside railing until my knuckles turned white as we torpedoed away from the docks. I stole a glance at the odometer and squeezed my eyes shut when I saw the needle quickly moving past fifty. Eddie drove boats like he drove cars.

Fast.

After a few minutes of pure terror, I had to do something before my heart went into cardiac arrest. *Eddie,* I telepathically asked, *do you mind slowing down just a tad?*

The vampire didn't hear me. He was too busy fiddling around with the GPS. The needle was moving past seventy.

"Eddie! Eddie!" I shouted over the roar of the engine. A bright red buoy popped right in front of us. "Buoy!"

"What?" He glanced up and wrenched the wheel to the left. A huge spray of water drenched me but not Eddie. I felt like I was sitting in the splash zone at Sea World. "Thanks for the warning, babe."

"Can you slow down?"

"Sure." He threw the throttle forward, quickly cutting off the engine's power.

My head nearly smacked into the dashboard. "I said 'Slow down!' Not 'Come to an abrupt stop,'" I told the vampire. I rubbed my now sore neck. "Great, just what I need-whiplash."

Eddie peered out over the ocean with the aid of the boat's navigational lights. "I think I see the fort up ahead. Probably another ten or so miles."

"Great, but can we at least go at a normal speed? Oh, I don't know. Something below seventy miles per hour?"

"What's the matter, Shell? You never complain about the speed when I'm driving on land."

I glanced at the murky water. "I'm not a fan of boats."

"Really?"

I swallowed. There was no way I was going to tell him what happened at the docks. The boat rental was fairly expensive, and I wasn't about to make him turn it around because I had a sudden fear of boats. "Boats can capsize easily."

"I have had my boating license for a long time, babe, and I haven't tipped a boat over yet."

There's always a first, especially when the driver is going over seventy miles per hour. "Could you just go at a normal speed, please?"

Eddie gave a sigh. "Sure." He was about to start up the engine when we heard nearby splashing. Using the navigational lights, he searched the water around us. "Get down!" he said as he yanked me off my seat and dragged me to the floor.

I barely had time to protest when the sound of a shell being jacked into a shotgun echoed through the night air. A long, deadly harpoon made of whale bone whistled over where our heads had been. What's going on? I sublimely asked Eddie.

"Halt! Who goes there!" someone shouted at us. We cautiously peered over the edge and saw two mermen in. Merfolk look exactly like Disney cut-outs with two exceptions. They have gills on both sides of their necks and webbed hands. From what I have read, merfolk are a fickle people and don't care for land dwellers. I can't really blame them though. I would be ticked off at people too if they kept driving over my home 24/7. Apparently, Eddie and I had done just that. "We come in peace," I said.

Another harpoon sailed through the air in response.

Eddie and I ducked back down. "I have a plan to get them to stop firing at us."

"Okay," Eddie said.

"Sirs!" I shouted. "You are in violation of the Sapphire Sea treaty which states that the people of the sea and the people of the land are forbidden to fire weapons at each other."

"That treaty has been voided since your mayor died," replied one of the mermen.

They had a point. "Can you at least listen to us?"

"Fine. State your business, vampire!" they ordered Eddie. Did I mention they're a tad bit chauvinistic?

"We're heading over to Diablo Island," my fiancé replied, feeling not need to explain any further. Eddie and I had gotten on our knees and peered cautiously over the side of the boat.

"Turn around!" ordered the second merman.

"Why?"

"There has been too much bloodshed on that island."

"Bloodshed?" I asked. I wisely didn't mention the irony of their statement when they were trying to harpoon us. "What happened?"

The mermen looked at each other in feigned surprise. "They haven't heard, Klaus," said the first one.

The second gave a derisive snort. "Typical land dwellers! Only concerned with the death of their own kind. They could care less if a merperson dies, Gunnar."

"What's going on?" Eddie asked firmly.

Klaus waved his harpoon at us. "Our people have died because of you land dwellers."

"We haven't killed any merfolk," I said.

"Not you two, but other land dwellers have brought an evil creature to that island and have fed many of our people to it."

Eddie and I looked at each other in shock. Who would do such a thing? "What does this creature look like?" I asked.

"Some kind of water dragon with a long tail," said Klaus.

"Are you blind, Klaus," Gunnar snapped. "Its tail is short and it has brown wings."

"No, it doesn't!"

"Yes, it does, and it's green, not brown." They continued to argue about the description for another few moments. *Let's make a break for it while they're distracted,* I mentally suggested to my fiancé. I slid onto my seat.

Stay low in your seat, Eddie replied as he slid back onto his seat. He turned the key and gunned the engine. A wake washed over the surprised mermen. The vampire jerked the boat to a hard left before straightening it out as we sped well out of harpoon range.

A few minutes later, we arrived at the island which looked
even more ominous in the moonlight. Eddie jumped on the shore
and pulled the boat halfway up onto land so the mermen
wouldn't steal it and leave us marooned. He dug a couple of
flashlights out of a tackle box between the seats, and we tossed
our life jackets inside the boat. "Okay, Shelly," Eddie said, "why
don't you show me where you found those symbols?"

That same sweet, sickly smell was still in the air as I led
Eddie to the entrance of the large building. We made it down the
long flight of stairs without incident, and to my surprise, the
symbols were still there, alongside a glowing map stuck to the
stone wall. "This wasn't here before," I said as I tried not to gag
on the smell.

Eddie inspected the map. "It's a map of this island and
Zephyr. Look at this!" He pointed to the line that was drawn from
the north side of the island to where the Harvest Moon Festival
fireworks are shot every year. The nicer, safer part of the docks.
There is also an outdoor theater there as well. He tried to touch

the map, but a powerful spark of magic knocked him down. "Crap," he said as he scrambled to his feet.

My flashlight beam fell on one of the many symbols covering the wall across from the map. It was the same symbol that we saw on the floor of David's study. "Crap is right," I said. "I'm no expert, but I think the map may be protected by black magic."

Eddie sucked in some air. "You're right. There is a lot of blood here. Both of merfolk, Welkie, and fairy."

"All I can smell is that funky smell."

The vampire said nothing but squatted down to get a closer look at something scrawled near the bottom of the wall. "Shell, does this sound familiar? 'Fiend of the underworld, arise and do my bidding!'"

"The death ray summoning chant." We both fell silent for a few moments as we realized the gravity of the situation. Someone was performing black magic spells on a cursed island. That's never a good combination. "I think both Laveau and Mothman are somehow behind this, and David knew about it."

"What's your theory?"

"Well, the mayor is killed by a death ray, and both men are vying for the position soon after his death. David confronted Mothman about the death ray."

"Laveau's buddy-buddy with David one day, and then accusing him of black magic the next."

"But these candidates practically hate each other. Why would they be plotting something like this together?"

"I don't know, Shell, but—." He stopped mid-sentence as we both heard something big and heavy coming towards us from a dark tunnel. Something leathery and very scaly scrapped along the sides of the walls.

Out of nowhere a glowing yellow ball of slime came flying at us. "Duck!" I shouted as Eddie and I both hit the ground. It landed right above us with a loud, wet SPLAT! To our horror, we watched as the stone wall started to sizzle and melt. "I think that's our cue to exit!" I shouted as I got to my feet.

Eddie rolled out of the way as another flying ball of slime whizzed past by his head and melted some more wall. "My thoughts exactly!"

We both booked it out of the tunnel with the creature

gaining on us. I glanced over my shoulder at our attacker. The brown, dinosaur-like thing was football-field length and about as tall as a double-decker bus. Its huge, leathery wings were dripping with water as it ran on its four long, web-footed legs. I activated my shield bracelet just as a long quill from its short, spiked tail nearly impaled me. The creature made a loud, long sucking sound, jiggling the skin sac hanging under its jaw before a huge slimeball shot from its mouth, landed on one of the boat motors, and proceeded to melt one of our two engines. We were going to need a bigger boat. Preferably one with working engines.

"Shelly, cover us!" Eddie shouted as we dove into the boat. "I'm going to get rid of the melting engine!" With my shield protecting us, he shouted, "Duracell!" A huge ball of blue energy shot out from his hands and knocked the engine into the water. "Hang onto something!" He shouted out the spell again, aiming for the land by the boat.

A second ball of energy lifted the boat off the ground, and we shot over the water a good twenty feet away from land. A tidal wave washed over us as the boat hit the water with a loud thump. The creature gave up on us.

"That went a lot better in my head," Eddie said. His black curls were plastered to his head.

"And dryer, I hope," I said sarcastically as my feet sat in two inches of water. I bent over and wrung out the water from my ponytail. The only dry thing was the inside of the waterproof tackle box holding our keys and cell phones.

"Let's look on the positive side."

"What positive side?" I asked. "We were attacked by what I'm pretty sure was a Gojira and its toxic loogies. And I don't know about you, but I'm completely drenched."

Eddie gave a little smile. "We found out part of what's been going on here, and we didn't capsize."

Chapter Thirteen:
Here, I Come to Save the Day

When we got back to shore, Shamus was beyond

horrified when he saw the Hummingbird LX missing one motor. I

think he nearly inhaled his cigar in the process. Eddie managed

to calm him down by working out a payment plan with him. Then

Eddie took me home where I changed out of my sopping wet

clothes, showered, and managed to sleep for an hour before

getting up to go to work.

Before work, I flopped on the couch and turned on the

local morning news. The top story was a flooding at the civic

center. Apparently, a broken water pipe was the cause. "Both

mayoral candidates," the news anchor was saying, "General

Rufus Mothman and Leon Laveau were upset their debate tomorrow night will have to be moved to the Waterside Auditorium which was their second option."

Okay, that was suspicious. The civic center just happens to get flooded right before the first mayoral debate. I highly doubted the cause was accidental. Something was up, but I couldn't put my finger on it.

Throughout my work day, I tried to think of a way to prove Laveau and Mothman were somehow working together. Then it hit me while I was eating a dark chocolate bar. Quentin and I could go back to Diablo Island. I could take some pictures, maybe get lucky, catch the politicians with their hands in the proverbial cookie jar, go with Eddie to the debate, and expose the candidates before a live audience. All before the night was out. Shelly Anderson, full-time librarian and part-time hero. My first mistake was not telling anyone my plan.

As soon as I got home, I threw on my backpack with my sword in its book form, my camera, my keys, my wallet, and my cell phone and saddled up Quentin. The flight to Diablo Island took only fifteen minutes. "Are you sure about this?" the griffin asked once we landed.

I jumped off his back. "Yeah, it should take only a few minutes. Stay out of sight until I whistle for you." I tucked the whistle necklace under my shirt.

"Call if you need anything!" he flew off and disappeared into a clump of trees.

I took a deep breath before heading into the exact same building Eddie and I were chased out of. The only sound I could hear was my own breathing. Pardon the cliché, but it was quiet, too quiet. I took a small flashlight out of my jeans pocket and flicked it on. There was still a lot of damage inside the dark tunnel. The toxic boogers were now glowing a dull green. I picked up a little rock and tossed it at one of the glowing holes, but nothing happened. "The toxicity must have worn off," I said aloud to myself.

"Of course, it did, dreamboat!" Eddie's voice came from behind me.

I whirled around to see my boyfriend standing next to me. "Eddie, what are you doing here?" I looked at him. He was wearing a black cape. "What are you wearing?"

"You know how I like to impress you, my pudding pop."
Pudding-pop? Eddie would never call me that. I squinted to get a better look at the vampire. In place of his green eyes was total blackness. "You're definitely not my fiancé!" I said.

"Correct." The doppelganger in Eddie-form reached out and performed some sort of Vulcan nerve pinch on my shoulder. The last thing I heard was my flashlight clattering to the ground as the darkness closed in around me.

I woke up and found myself tied to a chair. I looked around to assess my situation. On a small table, a couple of burning kerosene lamps sat, casting flickering shadows on the walls. It took me a few moments to figure out where I was. The sweet, sickly smell was very strong. At least I was still at the fort.

"Ah, our guest is awake."

Two men stepped from the shadows and came towards me. Laveau bent down and lifted my chin so I could face him. "I do hope Xerox didn't hurt you, Ms. Anderson."

"You can't keep me here or haven't you heard of

kidnapping laws?" I snarled as I struggled against my bonds.

"We should have killed her when we had the chance," Mothman said. "I told you she was trouble."

Laveau shrugged. "Don't worry, my friend. Soon, she may be useful to us."

"If you're expecting me to be your hostage, then forget it," I snapped.

"My dear Ms. Anderson, you underestimate me. I would never hold you hostage. I was thinking that you might be a light snack for my pet. I do believe you met her last night."

"That thing is your pet?"

"Oh, yes! You see, Darlene loves to feed on human-like creatures. She is very hungry, and I think you might hold her over until the debate."

I was more than terrified. This guy was a psychopath hell-bent on a mission. Keep calm, Shelly, I told myself. Find out what they're up to so you can tell someone. If I make it out alive.

"You had the civic center flooded, didn't you?"

Laveau laughed. "Oh, no! That clever idea was the General's. You see, the General and I wanted to move the debate to the open air theater."

"Why?" I asked. "So you can take over the world?"

"Not the world. Just this city."

Mothman grabbed the Welkie by the throat. "You conceited idiot! Why are you telling her our plans?" he shouted angrily.

Laveau pushed him away. "Rufus, my friend, what harm will it do? She will be dead within the hour."

"What if the vampire finds out who Xerox really is?" Mothman snapped. "Did you think about that?"

"The vampire won't survive, Rufus. Xerox can be very convincing. He was for my friend, David."

I looked up in shock. "You nearly killed David! You little hellhound!" I tried to lurch forward in my chair, but nothing happened. Magic kept the chair firmly planted on the ground.

"David Endora was getting too close to the truth, Ms. Anderson," Mothman said. "We had to dispose of him."

"What truth is that" I asked.

"At eight-fifteen tonight," Laveau told me, "Zephyr will watch as General Mothman and I will be in a furious debate about our opposing issues when an extremely dangerous creature will appear. The citizens will be rendered helpless, and the general and I will put aside our differences. We will work together and save the day from the terrible Gorija!"

"Wow!" I said, "I have met some crazy people in my life, but you two have shot to the top of the list."

Laveau smiled his trademark crocodile smile as he glanced at his watch. "My, my! Look at the time. The General and I mustn't be late for the debate." He opened a nearby door. "Darlene will be coming to visit you once she smells your fear. It was a pleasure to know you, Ms. Anderson!" He gave me a little wave just before he teleported himself and the general out of sight.

From what little I had read on creatures like Darlene, scientists don't know about their feeding habits, and there was no way in Hell I was going to experience it first-hand. I glanced down at the hidden necklace. Quentin could get me out of this mess!

It only took a couple of tries, but by using my teeth and tongue, I managed to retrieve the whistle and blew on it.

Seconds crept by slowly. Finally, I heard the clickty-click of talons and claws running on the fort floor, feathery wings beating frantically, and a griffin calling my name.

"In here, Quentin!" I yelled.

The griffin came skidding into the room and crashed headlong into my chair. Fortunately, the magic holding the chair down didn't knock me over. "Sorry about that!" he apologized. Then he realized my predicament. "What happened to you?"

"Less talking and more rope cutting. I'll explain later. We need to get out of here before Darlene arrives."

"Boyfriend's ex?" The griffin swiped at the ropes with his sharp talons.

My bonds fell away, and I looked around for my backpack. The doppelganger must have taken it. I sighed. At least my captors didn't know my bracelet was a shield in disguise. "Nope, just a flesh eating monster who flings toxic snot as a defense mechanism." I climbed on Quentin. "Let's get out of here."

Using my telepathy, I had located Eddie by the time we reached the docks. He was fighting my clone in the parking lot of the theater and was getting pounded. I instructed Quentin to take me there.

I activated my shield the moment I saw the situation. My evil clone was slashing at the vampire with long, metallic claws. The thing was even hissing and spitting at him while he rolled out of the danger zone.

"Duracell!" Eddie threw a powerful energy spell at her. Unfortunately, he missed as it somersaulted onto the roof of his car.

Time to take offensive action! "Head over there!" I instructed Quentin. "Fly low, but not too close!" The griffin did as he was told. Once we were about twenty feet from the brawl, I jumped off Quentin's back, letting out some kind of primitive war cry. I am woman, hear me roar! I threw my shield in front of me as I landed, to my surprise, gracefully on the roof of the car in a low crouch. As I came up fast, I whacked the doppelganger in the chest with my shield as hard as I could.

It flew off the car and disrupted a cluster of unicorns, giant birds, and other riding animals before running towards the debate entrance. "Eat your heart out, Captain America," I said as a way of congratulating myself. I slid off the roof of the car and faced my boyfriend with a smile on my face.

Eddie was staring at me slack-jawed. He didn't know what he was more surprised at-the fact I had jumped off Quentin or I had just walloped a doppelganger with just the aid of a metal shield. "I love you," he finally said in complete adoration.

I gave him a quick kiss. "So, how did you know that wasn't me?"

"Two things," he said as he held up two fingers. "First, it wasn't wearing your engagement ring or your shield."

"And the second?"

"It said it made me a home-cooked picnic dinner."

"Ah ha! I told you that me being a horrible cook would save your life one day!"

"What happened to you?"

I gave him a quick Reader's Digest Condensed version. "Is my backpack in your car?"

"Yeah, your evil clone tossed it in the back," Eddie said as he fished the keys out of his pocket. He unlocked the backdoor and got my backpack for me.

I took out Knowledge, changed it into the sword, and clipped it onto one of my belt loops. "What I don't get is how Laveau is planning on controlling the crowds."

"He will probably be using a mind control spell under the guise of charisma." Eddie looked at me and nodded with approval. "So, Wonder Woman, what's your plan?"

"How about storming the debate?"

"Sounds great, but Laveau is mine!"

We entered the seating area and froze at what we saw. Darlene was back, hurling her mucusof death at the crowd. But nobody was moving out of the way. It was as if they were frozen in place.

Eddie and I did the best we could, shoving people out of the way. Finally, they broke out of their trance, and those with magical abilities attempted to kill the creature. But nothing worked. Darlene was practically invincible.

"Shelly!" Eddie cried out in horror. "What are you doing?" On the underbelly of the creature, I noticed a missing scale. The fatal chink in her armor. With my sword drawn and my shield protecting me, I rushed forward and slid under Darlene without consulting my brain first. When I jammed Knowledge into the vulnerable spot, nothing happened. No dead Gorjia. No cheering from the crowd for killing the beast.

In fact, she squirted a ball of toxic slime at me, barely missing me as I rolled from under her.

Once again, Quentin decided to save my life. He came swooping down and grabbed my shoulders with his talons. "I should be a superhero," he said.

"All you need is a secret identity." I quickly assessed the situation. Quentin and I were well above the chaos. But no one could kill Darlene. People were dropping like flies. Then I had another crazy idea, but this time it just might work. "Let go of me," I ordered the griffin.

"What?"

"Just do it!" I snapped.

Once the talons released me, I dropped on the back of Darlene. Now, I was faced with a dilemma: The only way my plan would work was if I lowered my shield. No shield meant that I would most likely leak like a colander when Darlene shot a thousand spikes into my defenseless body.

"I hope you have a plan, short of getting killed," Eddie said as he leaped up next to me.

"I do," I said as we dodged a flying spike. "Stand back to back, and when I give the word, you raise a force field while I lower my shield."

"Is that it?" Eddie leaned back as another spike whizzed by.

"Nope, I'm going to take the head off this sucker!" We pressed our backs together. "Ready?"

"Ready!"

"Now!" I shouted as I deactivated my shield.

"Citadel!" Eddie shouted as he released a green force field in front of us. None too soon because Darlene released another group of spikes at us. "Now would be a good time!"

I swung Knowledge in a low, fast arc. It sliced through the Gorija's neck as if it were made of butter. A stick of butter made out of scales, bones, and muscles. The neck was the vulnerable spot. Who knew? The head fell to the ground as the creature crumpled to its knees.

"Jump!" Eddie said as he grabbed my hand. We landed safely and moved out of the way as the headless body collapsed to the floor. "I think you killed it, babe!"

I nodded. "I've found decapitation always seems to do the trick."

"Kill her, Xerox! Kill the girl!" said Mothman as he pointed to me. Everyone looked at him in horror. He had forgotten that his mic was still on.

"Allow me," Eddie said as he stepped between me and the doppelganger who was coming at us full speed. The vampire took a boxer's stance and cold-cocked the creature twice with a rapid right and left hook, one in the chin and one in the throat. It crumpled to the ground like a sack of flour and didn't move. He glanced at me. "I find sometimes might is better than magic."

Mothman glared at Laveau. A vein was starting to bulge in the general's forehead. "You said everything was going to be fine, Leon! 'Get rid of the mayor, and you will have all the political power you can imagine,' you said."

Laveau started whispering, but every word echoed through the microphone. "Rufus, you fool, people can hear you!"

Mothman pushed aside his suit coat to reveal a leather holster. Before anyone could stop him, he pulled out the pearl-handled pistol from the holster and pointed it at the Welkie's chest. "I'm tired of all your liberal lies and broken promises!" he screamed as he pulled back the trigger.

Laveau had no time to put up a defensive spell to stop the bullet. Blood appeared on his white shirt as he collapsed onto the floor. People stood in shock for only a few moments as the spell wore off upon the wizard's death.

Two uniformed police officers rushed the stage and tackled Mothman. As they were leading him away in handcuffs, he was screaming about how the world and their liberal agendas were conspiring against him.

I looked at Eddie. "Another reason why I never get involved in politics."

Chapter Fourteen:
The Truth Behind the Diablo Tragedy

About a week after the murder at the debate, Eddie received some good news. David was asking for us, which meant he was out of the coma. It was a Friday night when Eddie and I were ushered into the wizard's room.

"Hello, nephew," David smiled weakly. His voice was hoarse as if he was at the tail-end of a case of strep throat. But it was because he had just come off the ventilator.

Eddie smiled back. "How are you doing, 'Uncle David'?"

"Thankful to be alive," David said. He held up a trembling hand as he gave a harsh cough. He looked over at me. "The Camelot Society told me you were the one who advocated and helped to prove my innocence."

I swallowed hard. "Well, I knew you would never practice black magic."

He laid his head back on the pillow and closed his eyes. "That's not exactly true," he said quietly without making eye contact with us.

Eddie and I looked at each other in disbelief. "What do you mean, David?" the vampire asked.

He sighed. "You'd better sit down, both of you."

Eddie pulled up two wooden chairs with cushioning, and we both sat down.

"What's going on, David?" I asked.

He slowly picked at the edges of the bed sheets, clearly not wanting to tell us what was on his mind. A few moments of awkward silence passed before he spoke again. "You know the story of Diablo Island?"

I nodded. "Reports of black magic."

"During the Wixom War, I was a volunteer for the armory on Diablo Island. The army wanted two Welkies guarding the fort. We were surrounded by the Wixom navy who had wiped out everyone else in the volunteer army and had us surrounded. Leon and I were the only ones left."

"Leon? As in Leon Laveau?" I asked him.

He nodded. "Leon suggested we summon a death ray as a way to defend ourselves."

"But summoning a death ray is using black magic," Eddie said. By reading his mind, I knew the vampire wasn't angry at the wizard, but wanted to know why.

"I know, Eddie, but I didn't want to do it. Leon pressed the issue upon me, telling me it was the only way to make it out alive. I was a younger and much more foolish man at the time. By the time it was over, we had summoned three different death rays. I can still hear the screams coming from the men on those ships."

"Why didn't you tell the truth?"

"I know, I know. I should have told the truth, but I was terrified of what the Camelot Society would do to me. So upon the request of Leon, I stood in front of the press and lied to everybody, telling the whole world the Wixom Army was responsible for the death rays." He stopped talking as tears began rolling down his cheeks.

Eddie and I didn't say anything. He was so shocked finding out that the one person he always respect and considered a mentor had been hiding under a mask. I thought it would emotionally crush my fiancé, but Eddie kept his feelings in check and remained silent and expressionless.

"Mothman was in charge of the army and a good friend of Leon's. He promised not to tell what really happened in exchange for hiring an investigator to falsely the report about Diablo Island. I've regretted my mistakes all these years. Even my anonymous monetary retribution to the victims' families still hasn't eased my conscience." He looked at us with surprise. "You don't seem angry at me for using black magic."

"People make mistakes. But I think you should come clean," Eddie said.

I nodded. "Give the families closure by telling the truth."

"Are you sure?"

Eddie and I both nodded. "We'll stand beside you."

"Thank you."

"So, do you know who tried to kill you?" I asked the

question that I already knew the answer to, but I wanted to hear the wizard's side of the story."

"After what happened to the mayor, I knew both Mothman and Laveau were behind the murder, and I confronted them. But they denied everything. When the doppelganger arrived at my doorstep posing as a delivery man, I knew Laveau had once again conjured up more black magic. The creature forced his way into my home, but I don't remember anything after that."

I looked at Eddie. "Do you still want to ask him?"

My fiancé nodded. "David, you've always been there for me ever since I was turned into a vampire. There is one thing I want." He stopped and put an arm around me. "Actually, we want it. Will you perform our wedding ceremony?"

The next week, David went on national television and told the truth about Diablo Island. Eddie and I stood behind him offering our support. Actually, my purpose there was more on the moral support side. Eddie provided the muscle in case anyone at the press conference tried to harm David.

Honestly, I was surprised at the public's reaction to the

news. Only a few people tried to throw things at David, but my fiancé fended them off. Most of the people were very understanding. "It was wartime. He did what he thought was right," people were saying over the next few days. The apologetic letters he sent to each family member of the dead soldiers were well received. I hoped they all experienced some kind of closure. I know David did.

A few weeks later, I was at Eddie's house writing out addresses for the wedding invitations when I received the phone call from Robin. "What's up?" I asked my brother.

"Now, I don't want you getting worried or anything," Robin said. "It's a possible computer glitch."

"What's going on, Robin?" I asked.

Eddie was retrieving a couple of cans of soda from the fridge and looked up when he heard my concerned voice. "What's going on, Shelly?"

"I'm with Eddie right now," I said into the phone. "Can I put you on speaker phone?"

"Sure."

I did so, and Eddie and I both sat down at the kitchen counter. "Okay, Robin, We're ready."

"Like I said, it's most likely some kind of glitch in our system. Remember those pictures of you from Barbara Spellman's cameras?"

"Yes," I said slowly as Eddie took my hand. "It looks like someone hacked into our electronic computer files and deleted all of those pictures."

I gasped in shock. "Are you sure?"

"We're looking into it. Don't worry about it, Shelly. What probably happened was one of the officers accidentally downloaded a computer virus, and it got into our files."

"Do you think it'll be a problem?" Eddie asked my brother.

"No, I don't think so. I just found it odd that the only file deleted was those pictures."

"Okay, Robin," I said. "Thanks for letting us know."

"Bye, guys," Robin hung up the phone.

I looked at Eddie. "What do you think?"

"I think you shouldn't worry about it right now," the vampire replied as he gave me a peck on the cheek. "At least they're gone."

"You're right, Eddie," I replied as I went back to working on the addresses and pushed this information to the back of my mind. This little mystery would probably never be solved, but I couldn't worry about that right now. I had bigger problems to solve. Like picking out a flavor for our wedding cake!

COMING SOON

Legacy of the Undead

My Life Among the Undead:

Book Eight

By
Camara M. Bragdon

Shelly Van Helsing is enjoying her new-married life with vampire

Eddie Van Helsing. When she is viciously turned into a vampire

by an assassin, her life is turned completely upside-down.

Shelly's strange childhood nightmares begin to resurface again,

along with dreams about an unknown woman who wants Shelly

dead. Who is the mystery woman, and why is Shelly her target?

Shocking family secrets are about to be revealed, and Shelly and

Eddie must make a life-changing decision.

ABOUT THE AUTHOR

Camara Bragdon has her master's degree in library and information science and lives in Maine. This is the seventh book in her vampire series, *My Life Among the Undead*. Visit her website at www.camarambragdonauthor.com

www.ingramcontent.com/pod-product-compliance
Lightning Source LLC
Chambersburg PA
CBHW041052310726
48978CB00011BA/526